Murder is the Only Option
Phillip Strang

ALSO BY PHILLIP STRANG

DEATH UNHOLY

MURDER IN LITTLE VENICE

MURDER IS ONLY A NUMBER

MURDER HOUSE

MURDER IS A TRICKY BUSINESS

MURDER WITHOUT REASON

THE HABERMAN VIRUS

MALIKA'S REVENGE

HOSTAGE OF ISLAM

PRELUDE TO WAR

Copyright Page

Dedication

For Elli and Tais who both had the perseverance to make me sit down and write.

Chapter 1

Nobody ever doubted that Big Greg was anything other than an educated man. In the homeless shelter where he occasionally bedded down, he had become something of a legend with his reciting poetry as well as occasionally playing an old, out-of-tune piano that sat forlornly in one corner of the main room.

He didn't often grace the premises with his presence, preferring on most nights to find a spot under a bridge not far from Paddington Station, with heat from a fire in an old metal dustbin.

Big Greg would not have been in the shelter that night under normal circumstances, but the weather had gone against him. It was the beginning of November, and for London it was cold.

Those who knew him would tell you that he was a cheerful man, always ready with a good story and a smile. Not that any of them knew much about him. There were some things that he never spoke about: where he had come from, what his real name was, and why he was on the street. It didn't concern Big Greg, a title he had been given in part because he was tall, in part because of his commanding voice. Many on the street looked to him for assistance whenever the police came to move them on, or the social services wanted them to get a job.

Big Greg, a man who apparently enjoyed living on the street, showed none of the vices that afflicted so many others.

There was never a time when he could be found drinking a bottle of cheap alcohol. Those who knew him estimated his age at between fifty-five and sixty, but even that was unreliable as he had an unkempt beard and a closer examination was not possible.

'What is it with you, Big Greg?' one of his street-dwelling friends asked.

'I mind my own business. I suggest you do the same.' It was the standard reply from the man that most regarded as a friend, even if his smell could be off-putting at times, the main reason that the local homeless charity was reluctant to allow him to stay for more than the one night at a time. One of their rules, archaic according to Big Greg, was that every person who stayed there had to have a shower, with plenty of soap, and clean clothes. Even though the charity offered to take his clothes, threadbare and worn-out with patches covering the holes, and to wash them for him, he always refused.

Any questions about why he did not want the benefit of their assistance were always met with the standard reply: 'I mind my own business, I suggest you do the same.'

As far as anyone knew, Big Greg had been on the street for more than ten years, and in all that time no one had broken through his shield. Bob Robertson, the manager of the charity, where Big Greg came every day for a midday meal, knew him better than most.

He would have told you that Big Greg probably had a secret, like almost everyone on the street did. With some it was a violent relationship, with others it was drugs or drink, but with Big Greg, there was apparently nothing. The man didn't smoke or drink, and he certainly did not use drugs. The only vice that he would have agreed to was a propensity to read, and he could always be found with a book or two in his hand. Also, others had noticed him writing in a notebook. Once it was filled, he would start another, discarding the old one in a bin.

Nobody knew why, not even Bob Robertson, and he had asked him enough times.

Robertson had once taken one of the discarded notebooks from a bin and read through it. Even he, a literate and educated man, had difficulty understanding what was written. All that he could see were disconnected paragraphs of five hundred words or so, with complex mathematical formulas and technical drawings.

He knew that an admittance that he had read some of Big Greg's writing would have been met with a rebuke, although he was curious to know more.

Robertson had run the charity for fifteen years. During that time, he had met a disparate group of people, but no one like the big man who every day presented himself at the charity's premises. There, he helped himself to two helpings of whatever food and drink were on offer. Some days it would be meat, others fish, even a good salad on one occasion, but that had not gone down well with those who ate only one meal a day. But with Big Greg there was no complaining. He came in, loaded up his plate, spoke congenially to everyone, and then left. No fuss, no fanfare, no interest in anything else.

The last time, Robertson had stood to one side of the room where the street dwellers ate. He studied the man that intrigued him. There was no question in his mind that Big Greg had a story to tell, a story so shocking that the stories of the others who relied on the charity would pale in comparison.

What did he know about Big Greg, Robertson thought as he sat in front of his computer: tall, well-spoken, obviously educated and articulate, and able to recite poetry, Shakespeare mainly, although also the other English poets of note, and then the man could write mathematical formulas that he could not understand.

Robertson entered one of the formulas from the notebook he had kept into the computer, and pressed search: no success. He entered two others with the same result. The fourth time, a result. Robertson looked at the screen, attempting to understand what it was telling him. The mathematical paper that he had discovered was far too complicated for him.

With no more to do, Robertson left his office and walked outside into the street. It was ten in the evening, and for once the area outside the charity's premises was quiet, save for a couple of the homeless dossing down for the night, wrapped in blankets, the ubiquitous shopping trolleys full of their possessions and whatever else they had picked up off the street nearby.

A man came close to Robertson's left-hand side as he rounded a corner. 'You've been spying on me,' he said.

'Big Greg, I never expected to see you around here at this time of night.'

'I've told you enough times.'

'I've no idea what you're talking about,' Robertson replied. He looked up at the man, only to see a metal pole coming down at him. Robertson fell down, cracking his head against a concrete kerb. The two vagrants, no more than twenty feet away, did not even look in the direction of the noise. If they had, they would have seen a dead body, another man walking away.

***

Inside Bob Robertson's hostel, most had been asleep, although one, a woman in her late thirties, struggling with the pangs of withdrawal from a drug habit that had blighted her life, had been fluctuating between sleep and wakefulness.

The woman, Katrina Ireland, had led a troubled life: an abusive father and an equally abusive boyfriend who had introduced her to drugs and eventual prostitution, but now she was trying to wean herself off the drugs. Robertson had taken her under his wing, as he did with so many others. During the day, she attended a clinic in the morning to assist with her drug dependency, and in the afternoon, she helped out with stacking the shelves at a local supermarket. It wasn't much of a life, she knew that, but considering the options she didn't complain.

Regardless, she knew it was not too late to make something of her life, and because of Bob Robertson, a man she admired, her future looked brighter than it had for a long time, but the drugs were still proving difficult. To her, they had been so seductive, and she knew that the urge for them would never fade. She was planning to move into a small flat in the next few weeks and the idea frightened her. In the hostel she felt safe, and as long as Bob Robertson was around, there was always a willing ear, someone who understood.

Katrina, awake and eventually tiring of a never-ending knocking on the door and abusive shouting, got up from her bed and walked down the two flights of stairs to the back door of the building. 'It's three in the morning,' she shouted.

'I need a bed.'

'Come back later. Bob's asleep.'

Katrina recognised the voice, one of the men usually huddled around an open fire on the abandoned building site no more than three hundred yards from the hostel. 'Are you drunk?' she questioned the man, knowing full well Bob Robertson's policy on alcohol.

'I've not touched a drop.'

'Very well.' Katrina opened the door. On the other side stood a small, hunched-over man, a blanket wrapped around him. 'Doug, what is it?' she said.

'The police moved us on. I need a bed.'

'It'll be daylight in a few more hours.'

'It's not the first time I've come late,' Doug said. Katrina had known him for a few years, and he was not a man who drank much, other than to keep warm. Most times, he just wandered around the area, minding his own business, looking in shop windows, ferreting through rubbish bins looking for food, and picking up discarded cigarettes from the ground. Bob Robertson, she knew, would not have a problem with Doug, one of the more harmless.

'Okay, but you'll need to be quiet.'

'As quiet as a mouse, you know me.'

The two walked back up the stairs to where there was a spare bed. Katrina knew that Bob would want to sign him in, and he'd not complain if she knocked on his door to tell him that Doug was staying the night. 'Bob,' she said as she gently tapped on his door.

It was unusual that he had not opened the door to Doug, and as far as Katrina could remember, it was the first time that he had failed to do so. She checked in his bedroom, no Bob. She walked around the hostel after making sure that Doug was bedded down.

Eventually, she decided to look around the adjoining streets. As she rounded the front of the hostel, she saw him lying on the ground. 'Bob, what is it?' Katrina shook him, no response. 'Help,' she shouted.

The two men who had been sleeping nearby stirred. 'Keep quiet, we're trying to sleep,' one of them said. The other raised his head, looked at the woman apparently hovering over another man sleeping rough.

'He's dead,' Katrina shouted.

The first of the men came over, his blankets still draped around him. He smelt awful, the reason that Bob had not let him in that night. 'Call the police in the morning. They'll deal with it.'

'It's Bob.'

'The hostel manager?'

'We need an ambulance now.'

'In the morning,' the vacant reply. 'I need to sleep.' The man went back to where he had been sleeping. Katrina, frantic and unable to concentrate, the withdrawal symptoms exacerbated by the stress of the situation, shouted at the top of her voice. 'Help!'

A couple out walking their dog, even though it was very early, came over to see what the disturbance was about.

'He's dead.' Katrina pointed to the man on the ground.

The man bent down close to the body. 'He's been smashed across the back of the head,' he said.

The man's wife made a phone call to emergency services. Ten minutes later, an ambulance arrived. The police were already on the scene. Detective Chief Inspector Isaac Cook, woken from his sleep, was on the way.

Chapter 2

By the time, DCI Isaac Cook arrived at the crime scene, the uniforms had taped off the area. The two men sleeping rough not far from the body were sitting up and semi-coherent. Sergeant Wendy Gladstone and Detective Inspector Larry Hill were also on their way. Isaac knew that the death of Bob Robertson would send shock waves throughout the community.

Isaac had met the man on many occasions, shared the occasional coffee at a local café, never alcohol. Isaac knew the man was a recovering alcoholic, probably the reason he could be so empathic with the people at the hostel. Whatever the reason, Robertson had been able to secure the patronage of a couple of the leading businessmen in the area, as well as the local church's assistance in setting up the hostel. It wasn't in the greatest of locations, but it was central to where the majority of the homeless congregated. As a favour Robertson had rounded up those sleeping in the park opposite Isaac's flat, although two nights later they were back. 'Not much I can do,' Robertson had admitted.

The DCI also knew Katrina Ireland, although when they had first met she had been Kat and she had been hawking her wares. Isaac had seen her at the hostel a few times; he never felt the need to remind her that he had arrested her when she had been underage and he had been in uniform. The woman in front of him at the crime scene, distraught as could be expected given that she owed her life to Bob Robertson, was not the same person that he had known previously. The marks on her arms were still visible from when she had injected herself, the tattoos still obtrusive, although now they were concealed by a coat. He had to admit that her attractive looks had returned, although she still had the look of someone who had led a rough life.

'You found the body?' Isaac asked, back in the confines of the hostel. Most of the patrons were now out on the street, huddled in blankets, some with bare feet, some upset, some of the others not conscious of what had happened.

'Yes,' Katrina Ireland said.

'Are you able to talk?'

'I suppose so.'

'I knew Bob well, if that helps,' Isaac said.

'I've seen you with him. You don't remember me, do you?'

'I've always assumed you'd prefer to forget the past.'

'Thanks. You're right, the past is the past. Bob had found me a place to stay, and I'm clean.'

'Difficult?'

'Always, but I was going to stay clean, and no more selling myself. I wouldn't have wanted to disappoint Bob, and now he's gone.'

'The best we can do is to find out who did this.'

'I had let Doug in the back door.'

'Doug?'

'He's one of the regulars. He's harmless.'

'What's his story?'

'I've no idea. You'll need to ask him.'

'Let's go back to after you had let Doug in.'

'Bob always likes to know if someone's being signed in, regardless of the time. I knocked on his door, but he wasn't there. I know that he's pedantic about it, in case anyone is slipping in with drugs.'

'Then what?'

'He wasn't in the building, so I put on my coat and walked around the block. That's when I found him.'

'Out the front?'

'Where he is now. I tried to shake him but nothing. In the end, a couple with their dog came by and phoned for you.'

'The two men sleeping rough?'

'You're wasting your time. They're both out of it.'

'Alcohol?'

'Their brains are stewed. They'll not be able to tell you much.'

'I'll talk to them later. In the meantime, any more you can tell me? Any enemies, people with a grudge?'

'Not with Bob. He could be tough if anyone snuck in here with drugs or alcohol, and there's a few who are not allowed in, but killing the man, I don't think so.'

'Will you be alright, no relapse?'

'Bob wouldn't like it. I'll stay clean in his honour. And besides, someone needs to keep this place running.'

'If you need any help, let me know.'

'I will. Thank you for not recognising me.'

'As you said, the past is the past. What you make of the present is more important.'

Isaac left Katrina Ireland busying around the place, organising the breakfasts, making sure everyone was out at the agreed time and that the beds were ready for the next night.

***

There were few people that Isaac Cook liked more than Bob Robertson. In a part of town populated on the periphery by the wealthy, there still remained an unsavoury element hovering in some of the rundown parts of the area. In Bayswater, it was expensive real estate and people with expensive cars and expensive appetites, judging by the prices at some of the restaurants, but with Bob Robertson, his meals came free. As far as the man had been concerned, your race, your religion, and whether you slept rough or not were unimportant.

Gordon Windsor, Challis Street Police Station's crime scene examiner, was soon at the crime scene. It was replete with the obligatory crowd of onlookers, the plain nosy and the disinterested, with nothing better to do than stare and offer comments, and a reporter from the local newspaper hoping to get a photo and a story. *Not a chance*, Isaac thought.

There were enough instant journalists with their smartphones and social media as it was, and the last thing he wanted was to make small talk to any of them or the local press, although he knew it would be required eventually.

It had been relatively quiet for a few weeks for the detective chief inspector, so much so that he had taken the opportunity to spend a couple of weeks in Jamaica visiting his relatives. He had to admit that a lifetime in England had not prepared him for the heat of the place, nor the hustle and bustle. He knew that he was glad to be back in London, but not to be taking control of another homicide investigation. There had just been too many, and even if he should be inured to the sight of a dead body, he wasn't. Not that Bob Robertson looked particularly distressed in death – he'd seen worse, but the man had been a friend. Isaac knew that the man's death was personal.

Inside the hostel, the uniforms were taking names and addresses, although most would only claim no fixed abode and a number of the names would be bogus. Isaac knew it would be only a matter of time before immigration was on the scene checking for any that had overstayed their visas. Under normal circumstances, Isaac may have been interested to find out if there were undesirables taking advantage of Bob Robertson's kind nature, but not now. For now, he had a dead body, and he knew that invariably one body leads to another. In that neighbourhood, Bob Robertson had been sacrosanct, the person you could approach when life was becoming too difficult or when your husband was beating you.

Isaac had warned him about covering for those who needed to be dealt with by the law. They had had some rigorous discussions on the subject of helping people in need, easing them through their bad times, criminal or otherwise, or whether they should be locked up.

Isaac never won the argument, and often he had to admit that Robertson was right. Better to have a sinner repent and not sin again than to have him locked up. That had been Robertson's philosophy, and in the area around the hostel there was not a lot of crime. The gangs maintained the peace for the man, the drunks kept their distance, and the drug pushers did not come within a square mile.

Isaac knew that Bob Robertson had been a pragmatist, always seeing the best in people, understanding the realities, and now he was dead.

***

The two men who had been sleeping close to the murder scene should have been the best witnesses, but Isaac could not place much credence on their testimony, even if they had been awake. Thirty years ago it was all too common: the alcoholic down on his luck, unable to afford to drink in the pub, relegated to cheap alcohol. Nowadays, it was hard drugs that affected the younger generation, and there were plenty of them making their way down the slippery slope from respectability to being degenerate and lost. The first of the two men, toothless and reeking of alcohol, was the more coherent, but even that was debatable, at least to Wendy Gladstone, Homicide's dependable sergeant. If anyone could make sense of the man, it would be her.

'Do you remember seeing Bob Robertson here?' Wendy spoke slowly, enunciating every word. Her Yorkshire accent still came through, even though she had lived in London for most of her life. In her fifties, she was the oldest in the department, and whereas she would not rise above the rank of sergeant, there were very few in the London Metropolitan Police, who could lay claim to her depth of experience. Isaac knew that there were none that could find a missing person as well as her. Back in the office, Bridget Halloran, the department's administrator, and Wendy's great friend, would be opening the case file, preparing a case for the prosecution, readying the ancillary staff.

Bridget, an avid enthusiast of the computer age, and Wendy Gladstone, barely able to write an email, had hit it off some years previously. Back then Bridget had been confined to a cubicle looking at CCTV all day. Wendy had asked her to assist with typing up her reports. Bridget typed at eighty words a minute, Wendy with one finger at a time. It had been Wendy who had brought her into Homicide, and after Wendy's husband had died, Bridget had moved in with Wendy. The relationship suited the two women fine, and although boozy nights did not interest them anymore, they were both pleased to pool their resources. With their improved finances, the boozy nights had been replaced by trips overseas.

'What's your name?' Wendy asked the man, who was sitting on a bench.

'Gazza, that's what they call me.' The man held his head in his hands, looking at the ground, not Wendy.

'Do you have identification?'

'Me? No. I'm Gazza.'

Wendy could see she was getting nowhere. Regardless, she was determined to break through. 'When you claim your pension, what do they call you?'

'Gary May,' the man replied.

Success, Wendy thought.

'Okay, Gary, what did you see?'

'With Bob?'

'Yes. Bob Robertson. Did you see anyone with him last night?'

'I saw the woman shouting.'

'That was later. Before that, did you see Bob Robertson?'

'Not me. I was asleep.'

Wendy knew that it was pointless, as it would be with the other man sitting alongside Gary May.

***

'Any luck?' Isaac asked Wendy after she left the two homeless men and returned to where Bob Robertson's body lay.

'Not the first time we've encountered their type, is it?'

'Not the last either. Did you manage to get any sense out of them?'

'Only that the one I spoke to had seen the woman who found the body.'

12

'Katrina Ireland.'

'You know her?' Wendy asked.

'A few years back. She used to hang out with a rough crowd. She was inside the building when he died; there's proof.'

'Is that what killed him?' Wendy asked, looking at the metal pole lying on one side, tagged and bagged.

'But why?' Isaac said. 'The man was well respected in the area, even by the villains.'

'DCS Goddard, what's he saying?' Wendy asked.

'He's already been on the phone.'

'The normal?'

'How he expects us to wrap up the case in the next couple of days. You know the rigmarole.'

'We've all been there. We don't know why Bob Robertson died yet, and there's no clue as to who killed him. Is it confirmed as murder?' Wendy asked.

'Judging by the size of the pole, it's a fair assumption.'

Chapter 3

The death of a well-known local person, particularly when it was violent, always raised the interest of the local media, but the death of Bob Robertson, well known nationally as much as he was in the area, ensured that the national press was soon on hand. Isaac Cook was not pleased about the cameras pointing in his face, the inane questions. 'How long has he been dead?' 'Is an arrest imminent?' 'What was the motive?'

Isaac was no stranger to the media, having taken part in more than his fair share of press conferences, usually with his chief superintendent. DCS Richard Goddard was a capable man, good at stroking the egos of senior management in the London Metropolitan Police, apart from Commissioner Alwyn Davies, a gruff unpleasant man. He had seen through Goddard in an instant, and the animosity between the two men remained unabated.

Isaac knew it was invariably lack of progress with a murder investigation that Davies would latch onto in an attempt to unnerve and ultimately unseat Goddard. Isaac assumed the present murder would be no different, and that in a matter of hours his DCS would be on the phone again, straight after a rollicking from Davies.

As Isaac could see it, there were three possible scenarios. One, Robertson had been attacked randomly on the street. Two, his death was premeditated, but that seemed weak as killing a man on the street, even though it was dark, ran the risk of being seen. Third, the attack had not been planned, but considered necessary by the assailant, and even then, there was the question of why on the street.

Isaac looked over at his sergeant, Wendy Gladstone. He could see the endless energy as she walked around the area, disturbing those sleeping rough, asking the inevitable questions.

He wondered how she could keep doing it, not showing the pain from her arthritis, other than the occasional grimace as she straightened herself from a crouching position. He knew that her condition was troubling her, and if he reported it officially, there would probably be a forced retirement, something he did not want for her. She had been with him for some years, and he had ensured that she made sergeant after too many years as a constable, but back then she had had a temper, told a few too many people in the police station to button their lips.

He remembered from his conversations with Robertson over the years that before he opened the hostel he had been a sportsman, although Isaac already knew that as he had been an avid fan of cricket, and the dead man had played for England on more than one occasion.

'Why a hostel for the homeless?' Isaac had asked him once.

'I spent a few years after my career was cut short out on the street, bottle in hand. I know what it's like.'

Isaac had not asked much more, as Robertson was not a man to dwell on himself, only on others, and he had achieved a great result. The hostel had been well run; he'd helped many of the downtrodden, even rescued a few teenagers from the slippery slope from ganja to heroin and the inevitable time in a prison after first resorting to prostitution and then to crime.

Katrina Ireland had not been one of those, Isaac remembered that. She had come to London from the north of the country. He remembered her when she had first presented herself on the street corner: in her teens, attractive, with dark hair, and slim.

The first time he had seen her, he couldn't understand why she was there, although it was not long before he had arrested her.

In time, he had observed that her initial sweetness had soured, and the fresh-faced look had been replaced by a vacant acceptance of whatever happened to her. He remembered the time he had seen her gyrating around a pole in a sleazy strip club.

15

He had been there as part of a drug raid, as it was known that the club was a front for distributing drugs around the area. He and a couple of other police officers had gone in through the front door, pretending to be paying customers, knowing full well that no one would be fooled about why they were there. Around the back of the club there'd been a frantic effort to conceal the evidence and to rush out of the back door. And that was where the other officers were, handcuffs at the ready.

On that pole, her body still lithe, her face vacant, her gyrations predictable, he could see that Katrina Ireland did not care. Now in her mid-thirties, her years of degradation had left their mark, but with Bob Robertson and the hostel she had blossomed.

Isaac had to admit that he had liked the woman's personality even when she was in her worst condition, and now, in the hostel, she was the model of efficiency. He wondered how many others on the street had a story to tell, how many others were once upright citizens, able to conduct themselves in the manner that society required. Some would have families who no longer knew where they were, some would have suffered tragedies, others would have been seduced by alcohol, and the younger generation would have succumbed to the readily available supply of drugs that would rot the brain and destroy the body.

There were too many drugs in the area, although it was not Isaac and his Homicide team's responsibility. That was for another department, although they were not having much success as the drug pushers were better funded, more able to operate outside the law than the police. Too many rules and regulations, Isaac sometimes thought. When he had first joined the police force, he'd been idealistic, but later he came to believe that following the book, ensuring convictions was paramount, but that the system was against the police. With a sharp lawyer the criminal would be out on the street again, especially if he had enough cash, the one thing that those involved in drug trafficking had no shortage of.

Not that it had helped Katrina Ireland the first time he had arrested her. The most she had to her name was twenty pounds and a black eye from the man who had cheated her out of the remaining eighty. 'The bastard screwed me and then refused to pay,' she had said.

It was strange, Isaac realised on reflection, that back then she swore like a trooper, gave herself freely to any man who had the money, even if they did not always pay, but with Bob Robertson in that hostel he had never heard her swear.

***

As expected, those on the street and in the hostel, were reluctant to give their names, other than the names that the street gave them. Gazza, Lonely, Toothless – these were not helpful in a case of homicide. Larry's approach had been to inform those inside the hostel that none were under suspicion, but their payments from the government were in jeopardy if they did not assist. Larry realised that most had complied, though some hadn't. He thought that one or two were probably in the country illegally, which made no sense to him. If they weren't taking advantage of the financial benefits of England's welfare system or working, then why stay. Not that he dwelt on the reasons why the people were in the hostel in the first place, only whether they were implicated in the murder.

Katrina Ireland was trying to get them out of the building, Larry was keeping them in. A few had attempted to sneak out of a side door, only to be stopped by a uniform.

'Did you see anything suspicious last night?' Larry asked an old lady.

'That's Mattie,' Katrina Ireland said to Larry.

'You'll need to speak up,' the old woman said.

'Deaf as a post,' Katrina said. 'She's got a hearing aid, Bob arranged it for her, but she refuses to wear it. And besides, she's been in here since yesterday morning. She won't have seen anything, and if she had, she's hardly likely to remember.'

'Why's that?' Larry asked.

'Too many years on the street, too many bottles of whatever she could get hold of.'

'Who here might know something?'

'Big Greg would be your best bet, but he's not here.'

'What do you mean?'

'He was here last night, but he left before lockup time.'

'Lockup time?'

'Eleven at night, we padlock the door.'

'Draconian,' Larry said.

'That's what Bob wanted. It can be rough around here; best to keep the druggies out, or else they'll be causing trouble.'

'You mentioned Big Greg? What's his full name?' Larry asked. He had spoken to the others in the hostel, at least those that the uniforms had managed to get some sense out of, and none had been able to help.

'Big Greg, that's all any of us know. He's here every day for a meal, sometimes spends the night here.'

'Alcoholic?'

'He's a strange character,' Katrina said.

'What do you mean?'

'Apart from his appearance, you'd not understand why he's on the street.'

'What do you mean?'

'He's educated, polite and speaks well, better than anyone in here, even better than Bob.'

'Drugs?'

'He doesn't even smoke. Bob never knew much about him, though they used to talk occasionally. Big Greg would help out here sometimes, although he could smell. I doubt if he had taken a shower for a long time.'

'I thought Bob Robertson was a stickler for hygiene,' Larry said.

'If they were staying the night. If it was just a meal, he'd turn a blind eye. And besides, Big Greg would help out the others on the street: read their letters if they ever received any, advise them on how to deal with welfare, even arranged for one of them to be admitted to the hospital for a hernia operation.'

'I thought Bob did that.'

'He did, but Big Greg could do it better.'

'Where do I find him?' Larry asked.

'He moves around. He'll be here for a meal later on.'

***

The team returned to Challis Street. Gordon Windsor and his crime scene team were still at the hostel, wrapping up their activities. Bob Robertson's body had been removed and sent to Pathology. Two uniforms were stationed at the hostel awaiting the arrival of Big Greg, an important person as far as Larry Hill could see.

Whoever the mystery man was, he appeared crucial to moving the investigation forward. Katrina Ireland had given as much information as she could, but she had been inside at the time when Robertson had died, and according to Windsor, a significant amount of force had been required to wield the pole that had crushed the dead man's skull. Windsor, as always, made his preliminary evaluation at the crime scene, although the Homicide team knew that if he made a statement, it was invariably validated later by Pathology.

'We need to go through what we have so far,' Isaac said. As the senior member in the office, he was also the senior investigating officer. For him this meant dealing with DCS Goddard, which he did not cherish, organising the team, which he enjoyed, and dealing with the paperwork, an activity that left him cold.

He regretted that his seniority confined him to the office more often than he liked, and he wanted nothing more than to be out there with Larry Hill, his DI, probing here, asking there, attempting to unravel the fiction from the fact.

'No one saw anything,' Wendy said, pleased to be back in the office. She was no longer always gasping for a cigarette after kicking the habit of a lifetime. It had been hard, and the nicotine patches had helped, although a cancer scare, eventually discovered to be a false alarm, had firmed her resolve. Wendy missed her husband, but he had suffered from dementia at the end, and Bridget, a few years younger than her, had kicked out her live-in lover after he had started to throw his weight around, expecting her to wait on him hand and foot. Purely platonic, Wendy told the plain nosy if they ever asked about her and Bridget sharing a house.

Wendy turned a blind eye if Bridget brought home a man, but it was not frequent, and there was certainly never a man in his underwear sitting across from her at the breakfast table. Sometimes, Wendy would hear her friend and her paramour in the room two doors down from her bedroom, and sometimes regretted that she did not feel the passion, but it was not a big issue. Wendy knew that a cigarette would have been preferable to a sweaty man anyway, not that that option was available either.

And besides, she wanted to stay with the police force, and it was becoming harder to pass the medicals. Apart from arthritis, her breathing was laboured due to insufficient lung capacity, the effect of forty cigarettes a day for nearly thirty years. She could feel that there had been an improvement in the six months since she had finally kicked the habit, and each day without fail she'd be out of the house at six in the morning for a walk around the block, no more than twenty minutes, but it was helping. However, with another murder, six in the morning would indicate the time to leave for the office. Isaac, their DCI, always preferred an early meeting to plan the day's activities, and this time, a friend of his had died.

She knew that the man would be upset by Robertson's death, not that he'd show it, but he was a sentimental man, a man she admired greatly. She remembered when they had first met, fifteen years previously, when she had been newly transferred to Challis Street from a police station to the north of London, and back then he had been in uniform, the same as her. Even then, he had been a good-looking man: tall, dark and handsome the apt description. Many times, she and Bridget had joked about his love life, and how they wished it was them on his arm instead of the invariably attractive female. They had enjoyed those nights out together, joking, romanticising, getting drunk, but now that did not seem so important to either of the women. Wendy still appreciated the occasional glass of wine, and Bridget would sometimes down a half bottle, but having to be helped into the house by a taxi driver no longer occurred.

Chapter 4

Big Greg knew that life was hard on the street, moving from one place to the next, avoiding the drunken louts who on the way home from the pub wanted to bang dustbin lids. Or else evading the police or sometimes decent-minded citizens aiming to help. Regardless of all the negatives, there was one thing that Big Greg knew above everything else: he wanted to be left alone.

He remembered the day well, the day when his life changed, not for the better, but for the inevitable. There were, he knew, others who were still looking for him, others who would take the information from him by force, others who would kill him on the spot.

If Bob Robertson, a friend, and Big Greg knew he had precious few of them, had not become inquisitive, then he would still be alive. And what if there was someone out there monitoring the internet? Someone so savvy that one of his formulas entered into the search bar would be triggering an alarm, an IP address, a location.

Bob Robertson had opened a can of worms, a can of intrigue and deception. Big Greg wondered if it would ever close again. He knew that he could be violent – hadn't that happened that last day of his suffering.

He remembered it so clearly, even though it had been over eleven years ago. There he had been, a member of a team attempting to solve an imponderable that had confounded many for years, still did, yet it had been him who had come up with the solution. He remembered those who had held him captive for the next ten days after he had refused to give them what they wanted, and had beaten and tortured him relentlessly, drugged him with truth serum.

It had been a feat of superhuman strength that he had overpowered the men holding him, allowing him to escape. There had been bad years after that, years when he could not communicate with his family, never let them know that he was still alive, although he had kept a watch from a distance. He saw them daily: his daughter now a grown woman with a family of her own, his wife with another man.

It saddened him that he had been forced to kill another man to protect himself, but it was the solution, contained in the complex formulas and the technical drawings, that was all important. He had considered taking his life, but that was not the answer, and if he did, then what? Who would keep an eye on his family, who would protect the people of the country from what he had discovered? There were others, members of his team, who were still working on the problem, getting nowhere, but if they did, if he believed that they were getting close, he would have to act; he would have to kill again.

There had been one, a smart young woman whom he had admired. Her genius level intellect was close to his. It was unfortunate, the day he had to push her in front of an express train as it passed through the railway station where she was waiting for the train to take her back to her small flat. That had caused him anguish for some months afterwards, but his secret had remained safe.

It had not been easy, after killing Bob Robertson. He had kept out of sight since then by hiding in an abandoned warehouse, scavenging at night for scraps of food. He knew the police would be looking for him, not necessarily as the murderer, but he had been at the hostel that night, and he had disappeared after the killing. He knew the police were not stupid, and that they'd put two and two together and realise that he was a principal witness. He knew that he had perfected his disguise: the beard, the old clothes, the rank smell. He didn't like any of them, but the alternative was not preferable.

The tenuous political situation all those years ago remained the same today. Some people would take the efforts of his research and use it as a weapon. The death of a few individuals and his less than satisfactory lifestyle were a small cost.

Big Greg sat in a corner of the warehouse, its construction half complete. He missed those who had become his friends, the downtrodden, the incoherent, the brain-addled, yet he did not know why. He had grown up in a comfortable middle-class household, shown brilliance at a young age, left Oxford University with an honours degree in mathematics.

The mandate of his last position in the government research department had been clear: the development of low-cost energy. Idealistic, he had thought at the time, but he and the others had applied their collective wisdom to the solution.

That had been fine for the six years they had worked as a team on the problem. It had been him who had come up with the final solution, the stabilising of the energy, the directional control of the microwave beam from the solar collectors in low-level orbit, and he was willing to reveal it at an upcoming presentation, including to his team, but then he had overheard their director talking in the conference room to some men in uniform.

Three men. One was the director of the government department where the research department was located, a decent man, idealistic, the same as he was, Big Greg knew that. The other two were clearly military. The discussion: the military implications of what he alone had solved.

Big Greg, although that was not how he was known then, realised that what the military men saw was that the potential of low-cost and virtually limitless energy could also be directed towards weapon development. He also knew that the director would be forced to hand over all the information regardless of his protestations, or else…

Even though he was now relegated to the street and its deprivations, Big Greg knew that it was a small cost if it protected those he held dear. If they, the scurrilous element in the security services and the military, knew that he still lived, then his wife and his daughter, even his grandchild, could be threatened.

'We only need the solution,' the lead torturer had said.

Big Greg remembered him well: short, swarthy, a London accent. The man revealed that he had been assigned to an army base in Egypt to oversee Egypt's treatment of Al Qaeda fighters they had brought in from Afghanistan. How he had signed the papers to allow the waterboarding, the electric shock treatment, the beatings, and the sleep deprivation.

'You've held up better than they did,' the sadistic man had said once. 'You'll not leave here without telling us all we want, or else it's your family. I've seen your wife, pretty isn't she, and how about your daughter? What we could do with them,' he had said.

Cornered, Big Greg was unable to reason with the man, to explain that what they wanted him to give them was too dangerous to be in the hands of malevolent dictatorships or governments; it was the ultimate weapon, that could generate energy for the betterment of mankind or to destroy vast sections of it. He knew they would not let him leave alive, and if his family were the lever, they'd use them.

Desperate, his ability to resist the interrogation weakening, he plotted his escape. Big Greg, taller than the average and twice the size of his interrogator, and with his bindings loosened after his constant struggle with them, grabbed the man that had been holding him captive using the last ounce of his strength and placed his hands around the man's throat. The man gasped for breath, attempted to break free, but there was no one else in the room to help him. Eventually, Big Greg placed him in the chair where he had been restrained not five minutes before and made good his escape, but not before maiming another who stood in his way. His only thought was how to protect his family.

The knowledge he possessed was too important; his family was not safe, never would be. The only solution was for him to die. This had not been so easy to arrange. The researcher's death was assumed, once they had found his clothes stacked on a beach and a suicide note posted to his wife, that he had swum out to his death. Not that it prevented them bringing his wife in for interrogation, a situation that he could not control, but it had not lasted long.

The body of the tramp that he had killed, a man with similar features he had found under a railway bridge, was not hard to deal with: a suitable number of bricks and the man had sunk into the silt on the river bed without a trace. For the first few weeks, the new Big Greg had kept a low profile, allowing his appearance to degenerate, his beard to grow. Once the transformation was complete, he had returned to within a mile of his family and had watched them from a place in a park across from the house that he had shared with them once.

In time, the hurt of seeing them without him had diminished. However, his daughter maturing, making a fool of herself sometimes, getting drunk too often, sleeping with the wrong man, had been difficult, but she had passed that phase and had matured into someone he was proud to call his daughter. Once, she had given him some money as he sat there watching her. 'Here you are,' she had said, as she passed by him with his grandchild in its pushchair. He had wanted to lean over and touch the baby, but he didn't. He knew what would be the reaction of the mother, his daughter, and it was best for all concerned if she saw him as an old tramp down on his luck.

***

Isaac and the investigation team met as they always did at the Homicide department's office in Challis Street. As always, the ubiquitous presence of Detective Chief Superintendent Goddard, the demand to wrap up the case as soon as possible, which to Isaac seemed yet again to be rhetoric over reality. So far, they had a body, no motive, and certainly no murderer. The fingerprints, according to Gordon Windsor, the CSE, had revealed nothing of value. It was likely due to the cold evening that whoever had wielded the pole had worn gloves.

'Why Bob Robertson?' Wendy Gladstone asked.

'Why not?' DI Larry Hill said. 'The man must have had enemies, the same as all of us.'

'Did he?' Isaac asked. He had just had two weeks in Jamaica, his parents had come from there, visiting relatives, soaking up the sun, eating chicken jerk in Boston Bay, jumping off the cliff into the sea at Negril, and chasing a few too many of the dusky maidens, yet a murder investigation gave him more pleasure.

Most people would have thought him crazy to find joy in dealing with the underbelly of society, and now in this case, the homeless, but for Isaac that was the real world, not the sun-soaked paradise, although his parents' homeland had more than its fair share of drug-related crime, including the drug mules taking the drugs into the UK. His team had become heavily involved with drugs, mainly heroin, in a previous case, after a dismembered corpse had been pulled out of the canal in Little Venice. However, knowing Bob Robertson's aversion to drugs and alcohol, Isaac hoped that this time there'd be no drugs involved.

Isaac could see the beneficial effect Bob Robertson had had on Katrina Ireland when he met her that night, and there had been others who after a spell in prison had ended up in the hostel. Most of those had found jobs locally in Paddington, usually menial.

'What do we know about Bob Robertson? Isaac asked. 'Apart from the fact that he was a decent man.'

'Nothing,' Wendy replied.

'I want this wrapped up in the next week,' DCS Goddard said as he left the office. He had arrived looking for good news to relay to his seniors, not to hear a debate.

Isaac chose to ignore his departure. 'Wendy, find out what you can about the victim. Work with Bridget on this one. Larry, focus on Big Greg, find out what you can about him.'

'From what I've been able to gather from Katrina Ireland, the man is well known in the area. An anachronism really,' Larry said.

'Could he have killed Robertson?' Isaac asked.

'There's no reason why not, but where's the motive? A homeless man doesn't usually commit murder. It doesn't fit the profile.'

'What profile? As you've said, the man does not fit the usual criteria for being homeless. If he's educated, and not suffering from any addictions, what's he doing out on the street? He doesn't fit your homeless profile, does he?'

'Not at all. I'll check him out. He's bound to be known to welfare,' Larry said.

Chapter 5

Big Greg knew one thing, he had killed again and for the right reasons. Not that anyone would understand, certainly not the police and definitely not Bob Robertson's family.

Yet again he was forced to live with a secret that he had to keep. It was as if he had given himself to martyrdom, knowing full well that there would be no accolade for him, no sainthood bestowed from Rome, no being welcomed back into the bosom of his family.

He had seen his daughter again walking in the park. It had been dusk, and she had not seen him, not that she ever did, apart from that one time when she had caught him unawares. Even in that short period he had seen the kindness in her heart, in that she had been willing to donate her time, even some money, to an undeserving man. He had been careful to conceal his educated accent, to affect the voice of the street. Her best protection, as for his wife and his grandchild, had been for the world to believe he was dead.

His daughter was oblivious to what had happened, what would happen if they could use her as a lever to get to him, and they would. Now that Bob Robertson had entered those formulas into Google, the one place where the information would eventually be discovered, then what? Big Greg knew that Robertson's death had been a reaction to what the inquisitive man had done. Too little, too late, he realised.

He knew he had to do something now, but what? And as for the secret, they would kill for it, as would he. He knew it was up to him to act.

***

Katrina Ireland had always known that one day her luck would change. With Bob Robertson no longer in control of the hostel, the organisation of the place had fallen on her. He had suggested that she should become more involved once or twice before his death. The rental accommodation that Bob had arranged for her was no longer needed as there was always a place for her to stay at the hostel; not Bob's bedroom, she wasn't ready for that yet, but his office was free. Katrina took one of the beds from the main dormitory and gave it a thorough cleaning; it smelt of disinfectant by the time she had finished, but at least she'd not be sharing it with any other, microscopic or otherwise. Not that she wanted to either. Too much time on the street selling herself and then gyrating around a pole had tainted her desire for men, and then there had been Walter, who used to hit her often but he was now doing time in prison for murder.

She had admired Bob, probably would have been available to him if he had been willing to make an honest woman of her. She had observed that he only drank coffee, black and strong, although he would sometimes linger to take in the whiff of alcohol that was all too common on the street outside the hostel when the queue was forming for the free meal each day.

Not that she had formed an opinion of what he may have been. To her, the person in front of her was the person she knew, not the person they had been.

It had been the same with Walter, her last boyfriend. He had treated her well at first, knew what she had been, and he had been willing to accept her. With time, his passion for her had subsided, only to be replaced by a loathing of her past history. It had been on one of those occasions, after a particularly severe beating, that she had relapsed and had found the man on a corner not far from the place they rented.

It was only later when the police knocked on her door that she knew that Walter, in an act of anger, had killed the man who had sold her the heroin. She knew then that he had cared for her in his way, although mitigating circumstances that he had been protecting his girlfriend had counted for little, and he had been convicted of murder.

30

For a while, she had visited him in prison every week, but in time the visits had become more infrequent, eventually withering away to none.

One week after the last visit, one hour after selling herself to the last man, she had found herself in the hostel, with Bob Robertson on the phone organising an appointment for her at a detox centre and a place to stay for the night. He had even given up his bed that night for her and slept in with the vagrants. She never forgot his generosity, his willingness to trust a person who could not trust in return. As she sat in his office, she knew she would never let him down. The hostel had been important to him, it would be to her. She switched on the computer, noting the password written on a scrap of paper.

The hostel had benefactors, local businessmen who assisted with their time and their money. She needed to contact them, let them know that the hostel was to continue and she would be running it in Bob's memory.

Apart from the usual files dealing with income and expenditure, she found the phone numbers of the businessmen that she needed to contact. She called them; they'd be available within the next day or so.

Now firmly in control, Katrina looked further into the programmes on the office computer. It was clear that Bob had surfed the internet on a regular basis, some of the sites inappropriate, although she ignored those.

One site interested her, a site that dealt with mathematics, though she didn't understand what it said. There was a notebook in the top left-hand drawer of the desk that she sat at. She opened it. The formulas on the computer screen and in the notebook showed similarities.

***

Larry Hill made contact with the neighbourhood government job centre; a pleasant woman in her late twenties attended to him. 'There's no record of anyone matching that description,' she had said after Larry had passed on all that he knew about Big Greg. Larry found it strange that a man, clearly noticeable due to his height, could appear and disappear at will. At the hostel they had only known him by a nickname, and even the records Katrina Ireland had shown him confirmed that he always signed in as Big Greg.

'It would help if I had a photo,' the young lady said. Larry had to admit that he was enjoying his time talking to her. There had been another row at home again, the third in as many days, the subject, the same: his long hours at work, his beer consumption, his expanding girth when he was on a strict wife-enforced diet. Larry knew that she was right on all three counts, but he was a police officer, not a child, and sometimes he needed to let off steam, drink more than he should, and if that included a pub lunch and a few laughs, then so be it. He realised, though, that he should have kept the comments to himself. He had walked out of the house that morning angry, but as usual with him and his wife, their collective anger was short-lived.

He'd phoned her up after two hours to apologise, and said that he'd be home at a reasonable hour that night. The only problem, he knew too well, was the reasonable time promise. Now he had a man who needed to be found, even if it was only to clear him of the charge of murder: a man that officially did not exist.

He'd wanted to stay chatting to the young lady, but she was busy, as was he. She had a warm office but where he was heading was out on the street, checking all the haunts where the homeless congregated, it was not.

***

There wasn't anything that Isaac Cook disliked more than paperwork, and it always snowballed whenever there was a murder. He knew that he was lucky to have Bridget Halloran in the department, a dab hand on the computer, a paperwork administrator par excellence. He was aware that she could take the majority off him in the early stages of a murder enquiry, but once the missing pieces of the jigsaw started to be found, then he'd be taking a lot of it back.

He'd tried to get someone to assist Bridget, but the woman was stubborn, wanting to be the Mother Hen, not only of him, but of the office, and whereas some had come to help, most had not been suitable anyway. Only one had shown promise, and he'd soon left to take up a better position with Fraud. Not that Isaac could blame him, as the man was more qualified than the job required. And besides, Isaac had to admit that he preferred a tight, cohesive team.

He knew that with Larry Hill, Wendy Gladstone, and Bridget Halloran the bases would be covered, and none of the three would ever let him down. They were also totally loyal. He still remembered when he had been ejected from his position as the SIO as a result of the escalating murders in the Charlotte Hamilton case and the commissioner's attempt to bring in his man, Caddick. Though he hadn't lasted long, Isaac had seen some in the department sucking up to the new man, but his three key members had been professional, polite to him, but never sycophantic, even when their jobs were on the line.

Isaac knew that if it only remained at the one murder, then he'd manage with the paperwork, but experience told him there was more to the case than the murder of one man.

Isaac wasn't sure what would be relevant, but he knew that everyone has skeletons in the cupboard. What if Robertson had been killed because of those skeletons? It was a question worth considering, but first the department needed to find the primary witness and possible suspect, Big Greg.

Larry had spent further time with Katrina Ireland, Wendy had asked those sleeping rough close to the hostel, and Isaac had been around to the hostel on a few occasions before Robertson's death, but for some reason he had never seen the man. It was as if he knew the police on sight and made sure to keep away at those times.

Isaac had to admit it looked suspicious, but it wasn't often that the homeless were violent. There was the occasional fracas over a sheltered place under a bridge or next to a heating vent, even over a position close to an open fire, but they were invariably committed while under the influence of drink, or nowadays after taking illegal drugs. Even then, they were not injury inflicting, at least, not in the main, although there had been a case a couple of years previously where one of those being pushed had fallen into the river and drowned. Not that anyone ever came forward afterwards, and the homeless encampment had been vacated long before the police arrived on the scene, remarkable given that they typically moved slowly, always protested when being moved on, which was all too often.

Legislation recently enacted by the local council was disliked by the homeless, those who could understand its ramifications, as well as the protectors of civil liberties, in that the homeless were to be assigned to an area north of their current neighbourhood. There, there would be proper supervision, shower blocks, and medical care if needed. There had been protests, inevitable given the fractious nature of the society, by those who opposed it. Those who supported the move were the wealthy and those whose businesses had been impacted by a tramp sleeping in their doorway at night, leaving their makeshift bed and shopping trolley, even an old cupboard sometimes, for people to walk around.

Bob Robertson, Isaac knew, was one of those on the side of the disadvantaged, so much so that it seemed a possible motive. The man had not been the most vocal, not even the most influential, in that a member of parliament, a rabble-rousing individual by the name of Gavin Crampton, had taken the cause of the homeless and was using it to his political advantage. Isaac knew Crampton personally, having met him through the previous commissioner of the Met.

The former commissioner had introduced him to Crampton, unavoidable at a function to celebrate the relationship between the police and the general public. Isaac remembered that the MP had been sneering in his condemnation of any improvement and thought that the police were only there to subdue the downtrodden, to inflict their rules on those who needed support. The man was a bigot, Isaac knew, who had been elected in a marginalised constituency, one of the most deprived in the country.

Crampton, he knew, preached one view, lived another, and he was not to be found with those he publicly cherished, but privately was more likely to be at his house in Bayswater, or out in one or another restaurant around London, not that it stopped his proselytising.

Bob Robertson had been vocal in his condemnation of the legislation to relocate the homeless, even expressed his views on the radio, and it still remained a viable motive, but apart from that, there seemed no other reason. The building where the hostel was located hardly appeared to be a reason either, in that it was owned by a local businessman, the rent was paid on it, and the real estate market was flat. It could have been some other local residents who felt that their properties were being devalued, but Robertson had improved the area since he had taken over. Isaac remembered the adjoining streets from before, even though it was over ten years ago. Back then, there had been drug pushers who'd run at the sight of a police officer, teens shooting up heroin in alleys, prostitutes hawking their wares in the entrances to seedy buildings. Inside would be a room set up with fairy lights, smelling of cheap perfume, where the man partaking would be treated to ten to fifteen minutes before being hustled out into the street. There had been a disturbance where Isaac and his partner at the time, an older police officer, had had to intervene after the whore's pimp had wrested a knife out of the hand of a man who had just enjoyed his fifteen minutes' worth and subsequently found his wallet missing. By the time the two officers had arrived, the man had received a cut on the arm. All three, the whore, the pimp, and the victim, had spent a few hours at the police station before being released.

Katrina Ireland, Isaac remembered, had sold herself from the club where she had gyrated, sometimes from a phone number pinned up in a telephone box, although there were not many of them left, but never in a seedy doorway.

Chapter 6

Larry had spent two days visiting the local areas where the homeless congregated, even asking Wendy to assist him on a few occasions. As well as the two of them, Larry had also brought in a few additional officers.

It wasn't as if Big Greg was not known, as he certainly was, and by most of those on the street; it was just that the man was not around.

'He used to be here with me some nights,' said an old man who had found a warm spot around the back of Paddington Railway Station. Larry could see why, with a heating vent emitting warm air over those closest to it.

'What's your name?' Larry asked, not looking at the surroundings, which were grim. The man had an old dog tied on a lead; it looked as if it needed a vet. It had growled when Larry had entered into the homeless man's inner sanctum, a roughly constructed area bordered on one side by a shopping trolley overladen with at least one hundred plastic bags tied to it, holding whatever the man had picked up. Larry could make out scraps of food, old clothing, and a collection of broken toys, the refuse that most households discarded as worthless. The police officer knew there was no point in asking why the old man felt the need to collect rubbish. A person who slept on the street when there was accommodation to be had could only be eccentric or deluded. And the man that he was talking to, he was probably both, not that the dog seemed to care. It was just happy to make itself comfortable on a piece of old cardboard, ensuring that it took the lion's share of the warm air coming from the railway station.

'That's Bert,' the old man said. 'He's not stupid, knows when he's got a good thing.'

'Big Greg?' Larry asked.

'He used to read to me sometimes.'

'What did he read?'

'Anything that I had. I've a few books.'

'You've plenty of everything here,' Larry said. He was attempting to move away from the smell, but it was everywhere. Either it was the dog or the man, but then there were also the old bags, even some rotting bananas visible in one corner of the trolley.

'I always had a few books in case Big Greg came around.'

'Did he sleep here?'

'Sometimes, but most times he'd be under the bridge. They've got a fire down there, but I like to be alone.'

'What else do you know about Big Greg?'

'He doesn't like to talk about himself, I know that.'

'How about you? What's your story?'

'Life's easy, no bills to pay.'

Larry realised that the man showed the signs of alcohol abuse, a bottle in a paper bag nearby. 'Will Big Greg be there?' he asked.

'Is he in trouble?'

'You've heard about Bob Robertson?'

'Him down at the hostel?'

'Yes.'

'He didn't like Bert.'

'Does that mean you never stay there?'

'I take the meals, not that they're much.'

'Everyone else says they're fine.'

'Maybe, but I have to sit out on the street with Bert. No way they'd let him in.'

'There are rules, government rules, not only Bob Robertson's.'

'What need have I for rules? Bert doesn't cause any trouble.'

Larry realised that the conversation with the man and his dog was going nowhere fast, and it was typical of others he had

had. An unwritten rule out on the street, you minded your own business.

***

Big Greg knew that whatever happened the future was not safe either for him or his family. That morning, the third time in the one week, he had observed his daughter from across the road where she lived. He had wanted to tell her that he was her father, but he knew that was not possible. Her safety, as that of her mother, lay in their ignorance. For him, he could see no hope. He faced a dilemma.

There had been a progression in his life through childhood, then academia, and then a position with the government research department. As he observed his daughter fussing over her child, his granddaughter, he could see that it should have been different.

To work for the government on such a project had been inspirational, exciting, a great benefit to mankind, but what had it become, and why? He had been determined to take the project to the next level, to discover the solution that would ease the suffering of millions, but it was the men in uniform who had seen another use.

He had surfed the internet at Robertson's hostel using the computer in the cafeteria. It was there for all to use – he knew how to conceal the IP address – and it was old and slow, and the mouse barely worked, but it had been good enough for him to keep a check on the scientific papers related to the subject, and by those who had formed part of the team. Dullards the lot of them in his estimation, and judging by the quality of their papers none had acquired the additional intellect to complete the solution, a solution that remained hidden in his head and in a secret place that only he knew. If that fool Robertson had not been so nosy, he'd still be alive.

Big Greg knew that his death had been necessary. If one man had to die to save the lives of millions, then the cost was acceptable. If others had to die as well, then he would do what was right. It was a philosophy that had allowed him to endure the deprivation of the street, the foul smell that he oozed, the scratchy beard and the unruly hair, both which he wanted to remove. He knew that when the time came, he would do that, and he would reveal himself to his daughter and finally hold his granddaughter. His wife, he knew, was long gone, married to another man after he had been declared missing, presumed dead.

He wanted to talk to her again, to apologise for the hurt he had caused her, to explain his reasons, but that would not be possible. Those that had tortured him would be back, he knew that, and this time, they would be more violent than before. He had to protect his family.

***

'It makes no sense,' Katrina Ireland said. 'I need it to run this place and now someone's stolen it.'

Isaac had come at her request. He could see what she meant. The computer in the small office was missing, although the monitor was still there.

'I don't know why anyone would want it. It was old, not worth anything. All it had were the financial records, the ordering details on it. I'm stuck without it.'

'Can't it be replaced?' Isaac asked. He understood the difficulty the woman faced.

'I suppose so, but it's not so easy to replace the information.'

Isaac wasn't sure why she had asked him to come. It seemed more a job for a uniform. 'It must have been someone staying here,' he said.

'I know it wasn't.'

'How?'

'I saw who took it.'

'Who?'

I don't know who he was. I saw him as I was coming back from the shops. The man was dressed in a suit.'

'Did you run after him?'

'I tried to, but he jumped into a car and drove off.'

'What else can you tell me?'

'That's it. What would a man like that want with an old computer?' Katrina said.

'I don't know, but it seems important. What was on it, apart from details about the hostel?'

'Nothing much. I didn't use it apart from surfing a few websites and ordering for the hostel.'

'What did you surf?'

'I only repeated what Bob had entered in. Some formulas, that's all. I've no idea what they meant, but they seemed to be important.'

'How do you know?'

'They're in an old notebook.'

'Do you have it?'

The hostel manager – the title she preferred now, after the local businessmen and the church had endorsed her taking over from Bob Robertson – opened a locked drawer in the desk. She withdrew a notebook and gave it to Isaac.

'It might be important,' Isaac said.

'If you can understand it,' Katrina Ireland replied. 'It means nothing to me.'

'We've someone back at the station who's good with computers. She'll make some sense of it.'

***

Larry Hill finally returned to Challis Street Police Station, poured himself a coffee, heavy on the sugar, and sat down in Isaac's office. He had a resigned look on his face.

'What is it?' Isaac asked.

'The man's not around.' There was no need to elaborate on who Larry was referring to.

'I'm told he was always down at the hostel, but I can't remember ever seeing him,' Isaac said.

'Big Greg is a mystery,' Larry said. 'Everyone I met, and they all knew him, admitted that he was a strange character, and judging by the people I've met over the last few days, he'd not only be strange, he'd be off the planet.'

'That bad?'

'There are some sad cases out there, but Big Greg doesn't seem to be one of them. For one thing, the man never drank or smoked, and he'd sit quietly by himself, reciting poetry.'

'What sort of poetry?' Isaac asked.

'None that any of those I spoke to know.'

'Important?'

'It depends on what it was, I suppose. One of the men recited a few lines of one, "*half a league, half a league, half a league onward, all in the valley of death rode the six hundred*". I remember it vaguely from school,' Larry said.

Bridget poked her head around the door. '"Forward, *the Light Brigade! Charge for the guns! he said: Into the valley of Death rode the six hundred.*" Alfred, Lord Tennyson, it's the opening verse from his poem, "*The Charge of the Light Brigade.*" Surely, you must know it,' she said smugly before retiring to her desk, a smile on her face.

'I knew it,' Isaac said.

'I'll defer to your seniority,' Larry replied, knowing full well that his DCI did not know it either.

'What does it tell us about the man?' Isaac said. 'I've heard it mentioned before that he would recite poetry, and that he was highly educated.'

'It doesn't tell us much, other than his reasons to be out on the street must be severe. No one else out there could recite poetry to me, although one told me that he had been a schoolteacher until the alcohol had destroyed him.'

'Bitter about it, was he?'

'Too far gone to care. He'll be another one they'll pick up stiff as a board before too long.'

'Anything else you can tell us about Big Greg, a name possibly?' Isaac asked.

'I checked with the job centre, some of the other welfare organisations.'

'And?'

'Nothing. Some of them knew of the man, unmistakable according to those who'd seen him, but none could ever remember him crossing their threshold, hands out at the ready.'

'Is that how they see those seeking assistance?'

'Some do. One of the women at a welfare centre down in Holland Park was quite vocal on the subject, saw most of them as a waste of space.'

'It's hardly the appropriate attitude of someone in welfare,' Isaac said.

'That's what I thought, but then she'd probably had a rough day. Apparently, some of them can become belligerent, demanding their rights, unwilling to do anything in return, and, as she said, once they've got the money, they're out buying drugs or drink, but no food or medicine.'

'What did she say about Big Greg?'

'She'd spoken to him once, when he came in with another homeless man; helped him with the paperwork, dealt with the questions that she had asked of him.'

'Did she get a name for Big Greg?'

'She said he wouldn't give it, and there was no way she could force it. He wasn't looking for a handout.'

'The other man was, I assume.'

'Precisely. His paperwork was in order, even if the man wasn't. Big Greg dealt with the objections, clarified his friend's position and walked out of there with the additional assistance.'

'Big Greg take anything?'

'According to the lady, he asked for nothing, took nothing, and shook her hand at the conclusion, not that she appreciated it.'

'Why?'

'You've heard the stories. The man's hygiene was questionable.'

'Okay, no name, but what could she tell you?'

'She had to admit that he was a cultured man and that he spoke well.'

'Polite?'

'Exceedingly, according to the woman, and that he had studied the requirements, understood the responsibility of his friend if the money was to be given, explained it to him, even if he did not understand it.'

'This man's disappearance is suspicious,' Isaac said.

'Are you sure?'

'What do you think?'

'The man does not like questions being asked about him, he's not taking money from the government and any welfare organisation, and his real name is a mystery.'

'What are you getting at?'

'The man, for whatever reason, does not want to be found.'

'He's hiding out somewhere.'

'We need to find where.'

'He's still our primary suspect, hidden or otherwise. What do we need to do to find him?'

'Keep looking.'

'That's what you've been doing, you and Wendy.'

'It's not so easy when the man moves around, doesn't draw money from anywhere.'

'He must have some money,' Isaac said.

'Why? He could feed himself from Bob Robertson's hostel, from a rubbish bin around the back of a restaurant late at night if he wanted to, and as for clothing, he only changed it when it fell off his back. Although, from what I've been able to find out, it was probably welded to him anyway.'

'None of this makes sense, you know that.'

'Of course. The man's educated, articulate, yet he chooses the life of the street. There must be a reason.'

'Sufficient to kill?'

'It's possible.'

'We've a notebook that he had written in.'

'Any help?'

'It might be if we could understand what it meant.'

'What do you mean?' Larry asked.

'Apart from poetry, some from the classics according to Bridget, some of his own, there are pages of complex mathematical formulas and technical drawings.'

'Not my forte,' Larry said.

'Bridget is doing some research, not having much success.'

Chapter 7

Katrina Ireland, for the first time in several days, left the hostel in the care of one of the voluntary staff. Apart from a quick dash to the local supermarket, and the visit to a computer store to buy a cheap computer to replace the one that had been stolen, she had not left the area. Not that she wanted to: too many parts of London held unpleasant memories, and the withdrawal from her addiction still troubled her.

As she walked away from the hostel, not more than half a mile, she could see a couple – the man gaunt, the woman still showing some vitality – shooting up in a side alley. She looked at them, fascinated, noted that they were oblivious to her watching. She felt a yearning to rush down to them and to inject herself. Taking stock of the situation and acknowledging that she had responsibilities, she continued walking.

She passed the club where she had gyrated on a pole, passed by where she had sold herself, looking the other way. The memories were too vivid, too unpleasant. A voice that she knew called to her. 'I need that notebook,' it said.

'Big Greg. The police are looking for you.'

'They don't understand,' the man said. Katrina looked up at him. She could see that he had had a rough time since he had last been to the hostel, his clothes even dirtier than before, his face covered in grime. His hand was gripping her arm.

'You're hurting,' she said.

'I'm sorry, but that notebook's important.'

'The police have it. Did you kill Bob Robertson?'

'I had to.'

'Why?' Katrina asked. She had known fear in the past on more than one occasion; she felt it now with Big Greg.

'Too many questions,' Big Greg replied. The two of them were isolated from the people walking by, not more than fifty feet away. Big Greg pulled her to a bench and sat her down next to him. 'If you'll not run, I'll release the pressure on your arm.'

Katrina knew one thing, the man frightened her. In the past, the fear and the beatings were from a drunken or drugged man, even her pimp, sometimes her boyfriend, but they had only wanted to satisfy their lust or to shake some sense into her, or they enjoyed violating women, making them suffer while they proved their masculinity. But with Big Greg, it was different. The man was a murderer, had just admitted it to her. She knew that he would kill her if she gave him a reason. 'I'll stay,' she said.

Big Greg released the pressure, maintained his hold on her. She could smell him as he held her close.

'I don't want to hurt you,' he said.

'You've killed Bob.'

'You would not understand.'

'The police will catch you, you know that.'

'That's as maybe, but I must complete my task, protect others.'

'Others?' Katrina said. Big Greg ignored her question.

'I need that notebook.'

'What can I do? The police took it.'

'Then I will have the computer. You must bring it to me.'

'It's been stolen.'

'By who?'

'I don't know who he was.'

'Did you see him?'

'I saw him running out of the building with it. He jumped into a car and drove off.'

'Describe him.'

'He was dressed in a dark suit. Shorter than you, taller than me.'

'Hair colour, clean-shaven, walked with a limp?' Big Greg asked.

'He was running, so I assume he didn't have a limp. And yes, his hair was brown and he was clean-shaven. He was about forty to forty-five years of age. Do you know him?'

'I know who he works for.'

46

'Do you intend to kill me?' Katrina asked.

You must do something for me.'

'What?'

'You must tell the inspector you've been speaking to.'

'Which one? DI Hill or DCI Cook?'

'DCI Cook.'

'Tell him what?'

'You must repeat this exactly, is that understood?'

'You're hurting me again.'

'Sorry, but this is important. You must tell your police officer that he must not investigate the contents of the notebook.'

'He'll ask why.'

'Tell him that people have died for what it contains and that more will die, including the police, if they attempt to understand was it written, or if other people know about it.'

'That's not how the police work. You've committed a murder. They'll take no notice.'

'Then I will not be responsible for the consequences.'

'What are you going to do?' Katrina asked.

'You must tell the police that they are dealing with matters beyond their understanding, matters that will get them killed.'

'If you give yourself up, you can tell them.'

'They'll not believe me. I must remain free.'

'To kill others?'

'I must protect you and the others.'

'What others?'

'Thousands, maybe millions of people.'

'You realise that what you are saying sounds crazy.'

'If I told you, you would not understand. Why do you think I live as I do? Do you think I enjoy it?'

'I've never thought about it. Everyone on the street has a story, the same as you.'

'No one else on the street knows what I do. I suggest you do not leave here for thirty minutes.'

'And if I do?'

'I know where you are.'

Katrina sat on the bench as she watched the unkempt man move away. She could see his head down, his shoulders hunched. The man had sounded serious, as if he knew what he was talking about. He could have just been another crazy on the street, but she didn't think so. For whatever reason, she'd give him the thirty minutes he had requested.

***

Big Greg knew one thing as he walked away from the woman: he'd need to change. He had given a warning to the police, but no details. And besides, the details would not be for their understanding, and they'd only follow the official procedure of a murder investigation.

He knew that they would not hold back, but he knew that he had to do it, to ease his conscience. He regretted that he had murdered Bob Robertson, realising that taking the notebook and the computer would have been the best solution, but he had been angry that a man he had trusted had betrayed him. It had not been the first time that he had been betrayed, and would not be the last either. His wife had betrayed him with another man, although she did not know that. His colleagues, all those years before, had betrayed him when he had warned them of the consequences of continuing their research, and the young female had betrayed him by coming close to the solution. He regretted that he had killed, knowing that if those who had stolen the computer could be found, he would have to kill them as well. And what did the computer have? Titbits of the solution gleaned from his discarded notebook, useless to anyone who did not understand what they meant or how to link the scribblings to make them complete.

The only problem that Bob Robertson had caused was to let them know that he was still alive. They had traced the computer at the hostel because of a formula entered in the search bar; they would find him.

Big Greg looked at himself in a shop window; saw a man of the street, a vagrant, a person of little worth. He knew it was time. He walked away from the area and headed south. He needed distance, he needed another hostel that would take him in, somewhere that would not ask questions.

***

It was two hours, almost to the minute, before Katrina Ireland presented herself at Challis Street Police Station; two hours too late according to Isaac after she had recounted her story.

He had to admit she sounded plausible in that she had not been looking for Big Greg; he had been looking for her, and there had never been any suspicion focussed on the woman. Quite the contrary, in that even in the short time she had been running the hostel, she had been doing a good job, some said even better than the previous manager who could be prickly with those who did not adhere to the rules. Not that Katrina was a pushover, everybody knew that. Too many years rattling around the underbelly of the city, where she had encountered more than her fair share of gangsters, perverts, and malignant, misogynist men who felt they were doing her a favour when they gave her their money in exchange for using her body however they wanted. Some had wanted straight sex, some wanted to be tied up, some had wanted…

Katrina did not want to think about some of the acts she had been asked to perform, to inflict. Even at her most drugged, she had still known what degradation and abuse and violence were. Not that she had experienced them since she had cleaned herself up, and now with the hostel, they'd be no more. No more of anything, other than a life of contemplation, a life of peace, a life of serving the community. It was a strange feeling to her, and she realised that if Bob Robertson had not died, she may have deviated, ended up on the slippery path back to oblivion and self-loathing. She knew she could only thank the man for what he had done for her.

Visiting the police station where she had spent the occasional night locked up in a cell, to be fined the next day by a local magistrate, was not something that Katrina contemplated as her idea of fun. She'd have preferred to have not been there, but her meeting with Big Greg had left her more than a little disturbed. Whereas the man had not mistreated her, apart from his firm grip on her arm, he had been threatening.

He had a message, she knew she had to pass it on, even if she did not know what it meant.

'Please take a seat,' Isaac said as he welcomed her into his office. 'Coffee, tea?'

'I'm fine, thanks. I can't stay long, there's plenty to do before the nighttime rush.'

'What is it?'

'I've seen Big Greg.'

'When?'

Two hours ago, no more than half a mile from here.'

'You've taken your time to tell us. Any reason?'

'He asked for thirty minutes before I reported to you.'

'And you agreed?'

'I was frightened.'

'Maybe it's best if you give me the full story.'

'Okay. I was taking a walk. I've been in the hostel solid since Bob's death. I just felt like some fresh air.'

'Around here?'

'You know what I mean. Anyway, I'm walking down the street minding my own business when Big Greg comes alongside.'

'And?'

'He grabs my arm and pulls me towards a bench.'

'You resisted?'

'I could see the look in his eyes, and he was gripping me firmly.'

'What did he say?'

'He admitted to killing Bob.'

'Murder?'

'He said that he had killed him and that he would commit the same crime again.'

50

'He sounds like a psychopath.'

'He's not. I know what they're like, but he was sane, just determined.'

'But why murder?'

'He was very clear in that the murder of one or two people was minor compared to the cost of the truth. He called it the secret.'

'What secret?'

'The secret in that notebook and on Bob's computer. I didn't understand what he meant, other than he was adamant that you are messing with something dangerous.'

'I've seen the formulas and the technical drawings. None of us has a clue as to what they mean. Did he say more?'

'He said for you to stop investigating what they meant.'

'But there's been a murder. We can hardly walk away on the advice of the murderer.'

'I told him that.'

'What did he say?'

'He just reiterated what he had said before.'

'Anything else?'

'No. He left me there and walked away. That's the last I saw of him. He'd scared me. I didn't know what to do. I didn't want to come here, but it seemed important. He'll kill again. I just don't want anyone's death to be on my conscience because I didn't tell you.'

Chapter 8

With the admission of guilt, even if only to a third party, the department's activity to find the missing man continued. As usual, DCS Goddard was in the thick of it: advising Isaac on how to organise his team, phoning up Commissioner Alwyn Davies to update him on his success in identifying the culprit. Isaac, as the SIO, did not appreciate his DCS taking the credit, and besides, they may have had a tentative confession, but they certainly did not have the man.

Larry Hill and Wendy Gladstone were on the hunt, but there was nothing. It had been two hours from Big Greg leaving Katrina Ireland to her arriving at Challis Street, then fifteen minutes while she told her story.

By the time Larry and Wendy arrived at the bench where the murderer and the hostel manager had met, nearly three hours had transpired. Gordon Windsor sent over some members of his team, established the bench and the small park as a crime scene, and then checked for fingerprints, as well as combing through the uncut grass. They didn't find very much, other than proof that people did not clean up after their dogs had defecated when no one was looking, and that a park bench is a great place to deposit chewing gum after it's given all its flavour. Fingerprints had been thought to be a possibility, but none were found.

Wendy had organised some uniforms to ask around the area. One woman remembered a homeless man wandering down the road but no more, certainly not enough to formulate a direction and a possible search area.

Bridget, back at the station, put out an updated all points warning for the man, but the description of tall, vagrant, dirty, overweight did not help much, and no one believed it would come to anything.

'Stuffed it again, is that it?' Richard Goddard said as he sat in Isaac's office.

'Hardly, sir. We've got a confession.' Isaac had grown tired of his boss always criticising when it was not required. As far as the DCI was concerned, the case was progressing well. A murder confession was normally the last thing that was obtained, but this time the murderer had admitted his guilt without any coercion, which seemed strange in itself.

'You've one murder, one murderer. This is an easy one, looks good for the department if you bring him in.'

Looks good for you, Isaac thought as he looked over at Goddard, a man who had treated him well in the past but who now seemed more interested in furthering his own career.

Not that Isaac could blame him, as the man had been overlooked a few times for the promotion up to commander. The first time, it had been political, the highest echelons of government holding him back, but after that it had been Commissioner Alwyn Davies, a man who did not like sycophants or people smarter than him, and especially anyone who could threaten his position. Already, with less than two years in the job, questions were being asked about the commissioner's suitability, and not only by the rank and file of the London Metropolitan Police, but also by the mainstream media outlets, the newspapers, the television stations. After a couple of terrorist incidents – a stabbing frenzy by a group of homegrown militants when three people had died, and then a car bomb that had exploded in a shopping centre killing six people, one a child under two – there was often criticism of the commissioner, whose mandate included terrorism.

Isaac could see the problem, as could his super. Alwyn Davies had attempted to bring in his stooge, DCI Caddick, to run the Challis Street Homicide department, not because he was the best man for the job, but because he was Davies's man. Other departments had not been so successful in stopping Davies from interfering, and substandard, sometimes blatantly incompetent, people had been put in charge: Counter Terrorism Command, for example.

The previous head of that department had been pre-emptive, and although that approach had not always succeeded, there had been fewer attacks under his watch, but now he was sitting out his time in public relations, drawing his salary, and keeping his mouth shut. One politician in Westminster, well respected, had stood up at Question Time and put it to the prime minister that it was time for Davies to be removed and for the previous head of Counter Terrorism Command to take his place. The question had been met with a rousing response of 'hear, hear' from the Opposition's side of the chamber, which meant that the prime minister was forced to support the current commissioner. However, behind closed doors the prime minister had hauled his Minister of State for Policing, Fire and Criminal Justice into his office, and told him to make sure that the Opposition politician's idea was implemented.

'Just make it look as though it was our idea, not his,' the prime minister said. 'I don't want the opposite side of the House claiming credit. You've got three months, and make sure you put some tough bastard in charge of terrorism.'

Isaac knew this through Goddard, who was well aware of the situation, playing his cards close to his chest, angling to ensure that Counter Terrorism Command had a new name on its commander's door, namely Richard Goddard. Isaac knew the man would succeed.

***

As he had walked away from Katrina Ireland, Big Greg felt a great sorrow. It was not often that he showed any emotion, other than the impression of affability and contentment with being on the street for so many years. But he knew the truth: it was a veneer, necessary in its entirety.

He reflected on what had been, when he had been an upright citizen with a loving wife, and a daughter the apple of his eye, but he could only blame himself for his current predicament.

He could have just given them the formulas and the drawings, the completed solution; sometimes he wished he had, but what then? An accident, insufficient research into stabilising the weapon, whether it was used for peaceful purposes or not?

Liz Hardcastle had been a decent person, but he had pushed her in front of a speeding train. Bob Robertson had been a good man, but he had died at his hands. There would be more, he knew that, as certain as he was aware that those who had tortured him in the past would return. Didn't they have Robertson's computer? Proof that their monitoring equipment had picked up the formula that had been entered into the search bar.

There was one thing Big Greg knew, even if it cost him his life: he had to protect his family, even reveal himself to them if it was necessary, and inevitably kill for them.

It had been a long walk, twelve hours slogging down back streets, attempting to avoid the main roads, but finally he reached his destination, a charitable institution that he had used once before. He entered, spoke briefly to the man in charge, and walked up the stairs.

***

It had been three weeks, an eternity according to Isaac's boss, not so much time according to Isaac and his team. Since Bob Robertson's death, and Big Greg's admission to Katrina Ireland, nothing more had happened. Further searching by Larry and Wendy had found that the man was known in other areas of London, although for the last five or six years he had always been close to Challis Street.

Some others, especially those who lived on the street, spoke of him when asked, although they had not been able to shed any light on the man except that he kept to himself, recited poetry, and was forever writing. Big Greg's notebook had been looked over by experts, yet they had gained little from it, other than the formulas and the drawings were complicated, the meaning of them obscure, and what he had written was disjointed and fragmentary, almost as if they were in code.

Others, in a location some distance from London, were not in the same situation. They had the stolen computer, old and worthy of scrapping, but very little else apart from a formula in the search bar.

Katrina Ireland, the happiest she had ever been, had made significant improvements to the hostel, now named in honour of the man who had set it up. She'd even been interviewed by a local radio station, and although she had been nervous, she had done well.

She would have preferred it if they hadn't mentioned her past history, but they had. On reflection, she had to admit that it wasn't such a big deal: a woman redeemed and brought back from the brink. A local newspaper wanted to run a similar story, but she had managed to talk them out of it. Her past was behind her, and whereas it could not be blocked from her memory, she did not want to be reminded of it too often. One of the homeless men, after becoming aware of her background, had propositioned her, only to be evicted from the hostel.

She knew she ran a tough ship, but she also ran it with kindness; be nice to her, and she'd be nice in return. The local vicar had expressed concern about her past as apparently some of the old biddies in his congregation did not like the idea of a former prostitute running a hostel or of her taking church funds if they were available, but Katrina had met with them and they had relented, even embraced her like a lost daughter. Katrina had been moved by the women's change of heart towards her, as her relationship with her mother were non-existent and not likely to change. She had even started going to church every Sunday, the hostel demands permitting. The vicar quoting Luke 15:10 – 'In the same way, I tell you, there is rejoicing in the presence of the angels of God over one sinner who repents' – the first time she went seemed to be directed at her.

The first that Isaac knew of the latest development was when he received a phone call at home. 'Someone's been through the office,' Katrina said.

Isaac assumed it was someone in the hostel, but he owed it to the woman to investigate personally, rather than send a local uniform over. It took him only ten minutes to get there, as it was a Sunday and the traffic was light. He found Katrina out on the street, waiting for him.

'Anything missing?' Isaac asked. Apart from the worried look on her face, he had to admit that she looked well, a healthy glow on her cheeks.

'Not that I can tell, certainly not any money, not that there was much in there anyway.'

'One of your guests?'

'Not a chance. It's not that I trust them totally, but they'd be after petty cash, and besides the door is double locked and whoever opened it didn't break it down.'

'Anyone see anything?'

'Unlikely. It's the time of day when the place is empty. Those who stayed last night have gone, and tonight's guests haven't arrived yet. I had someone helping with the cleaning of the place, but they'd gone as well.'

Isaac and Katrina walked up to the office. It was clear that someone had looked through it, and they had been methodical. No throwing of papers on the ground, no rifling through drawers and spilling the contents on the floor. 'The computer?' Isaac asked.

'They've not touched it, nor the cash.'

'What were they after? What do you reckon?' Isaac asked.

'What you've already got.'

'The notebook.'

'I suppose so.'

'Are there any more?'

'I've not seen any. Do you think Bob was killed because of it?' Katrina asked.

'It seems possible, although we can't make any sense of what's in it.'

Even though the intrusion in the office had seemed minor, Isaac phoned Gordon Windsor, asked him to get his team over to check out the room. Katrina regretted that she had made a fuss as she had work to do, and the computer would not be available, at least not until later in the day.

'It's better to be safe than sorry,' Isaac said.

'I suppose so. What about Big Greg?'

'We're still looking.'

***

A smile crept across the man's face, and not for the first time. He remembered that first shower, the hot water on his body, the lathering of the soap. He had maintained his secret for a long time, but he had realised in that hostel that he needed to take direct action against those who threatened him. No more hiding away, no more sleeping under a bridge and eating scraps from a bin. There was money, he intended to use it. The case that he had taken into the hostel contained all that he needed. He had hidden it well for many years, and the clothes would suffice, although they smelt musty. He'd wear some, dry clean the others, and then swap until the process was complete.

He remembered walking into the barber's shop. 'Take it all off, trim the beard,' he had said. Those who had threatened him and his family would remember a man with a full head of fair-coloured hair, clean-shaven and a fastidious dresser in a suit. Now his hair would be cropped short and he would be dressed casually: a pair of jeans, a tee shirt, a comfortable jacket, and Adidas footwear.

He had walked out of that barber's shop unrecognisable, even to his wife if she encountered him, which she may well do if he was to protect her. He knew they'd come for her, especially after he went for them, but this nightmare had to stop.

Two weeks was the maximum time he had allotted for the transformation. Every morning, Big Greg visited a gym, and every afternoon he would run for one hour, as he always had in the past. The weight he had put on, at least forty pounds, would have to go, although he knew that it would take more than a couple of weeks.

The hotel where he was staying was of a reasonable quality, and there was a laptop in his room which he had purchased new. He was adept with technology; they'd never trace his logging on, nor where he was.

There were a few days to go, and then he'd deal with those who had been the bane of his life. He would do it for his family, for his country, but mainly for himself. It felt good to be back, he knew that.

Chapter 9

There was nothing that annoyed Isaac Cook more than a murder investigation that had stagnated, and the current case was par for the course. Yet again, a murder, a murderer and then nothing.

Apart from Katrina Ireland's encounter with Big Greg, there had been no further leads. It was known the man had moved south of the city after leaving her on the bench, as a witness had attested to seeing him shuffling along in that general direction, and then no more.

At least the situation was different to previous murder investigations in that the body count was not accumulating: this time there was only the death of Bob Robertson. The one advantage: Commissioner Davies had no reason to pressure DCS Goddard to pressure Isaac. In previous cases, the distraction of fending off criticism and maintaining his position as well as protecting his team had only hampered the investigation. Sure, criticism was always there, that was part of the deal when working for a large organisation, and if it's constructive, then there's always something to be gained, but with the commissioner and his lackey, Goddard, it was far from helpful and certainly not welcome.

And it was a Tuesday, the day of the week when Isaac would climb the stairs from his office with its view of nothing, apart from the windows of a building on the opposite side of the street, to where Detective Chief Superintendent Richard Goddard sat with his panoramic view over the city. In the distance, the London Eye, one of London's premier tourist attractions. Isaac had been on it once, taken an old girlfriend, but it had been overcast that day, and not only outside the capsule but inside too.

It was another failed outing with Jess O'Neill, another attempt at reconciliation that was thwarted by too much history, too many attempts to meet up, too many issues clouding the mind of the other. Isaac was invariably involved in a case, and Jess was always concerned about the next episode of the soap opera of which she was the executive manager, or a casting issue, or whether the decline in the ratings was permanent, or just temporary.

Whatever the reason, once the capsule had returned to the ground, they had gone their separate ways. It was a strange situation in that they still loved each other in their own way, but it had not stopped Isaac spending two nights with a woman in a fancy hotel in Montego Bay in Jamaica on his recent visit there. He had met her in Kingston, the capital of that vibrant country, they had hit it off and met up on an occasional basis during the two weeks that he was there, and now she was coming to London, supposedly on business, but he knew that she wanted to meet up with him again.

A holiday fling with all the attendant passion, the time to devote to the relationship, the lack of care about the cost, and the hotel in Montego Bay had not come cheap. If she was coming to London assuming that his lifestyle was five stars, his car a Mercedes and his flat luxurious rather than its modest two bedrooms, then she was in for a rude shock.

Not that he could blame her for wanting to come. Jamaica may have been idyllic for a tourist with British money, but it was a tough call if you had to live there on a minimum wage.

Wendy, his sergeant, was out of the office most days, attempting to find Big Greg, knowing full well that he was no longer anywhere near Challis Street. She was monitoring all those who approached the charitable institutions across London, although with no bites so far. There had been two false alarms, as a tall man from the street was not so common, but the first, in the east of the city, had turned out to be a man with a strong foreign accent, the second an alcohol-sodden illiterate, neither of whom fitted the description of the man they were looking for.

Bridget had compiled a case for the prosecution, which was tight apart from the name of the murderer. Big Greg was clearly not a name, and any attempt to unravel the man's secret had been in vain. The man only answered to Big Greg, not Greg, nor Gregory, not even Big, which created another problem.

There were registers of the homeless, the missing, filed by organisations and concerned relatives. Bridget had poured through all the information that she had managed to obtain, but even the name Greg was suspect. Larry and Isaac had discussed on several occasions what it was that forced a man such as Big Greg to give up a perfectly normal life and to take to the street, with its deprivations. One of the locations under a bridge that the man had favoured was neither clean nor healthy, and the smell of stale urine, stale alcohol, and faecal matter from dogs and people, not too careful where either deposited it, was overpowering. Larry had wanted to wear a mask in there when he questioned the people lying on the ground or propping themselves up against a wall, but that would only have raised their distrust. Those that he had found there had, bar one or two, given up on life, and as long as they had a brown paper bag with a bottle inside, or the opportunity to shoot up heroin, the discarded syringes testament to the fact, then they were fine. Big Greg had apparently not given up on life, and apart from how he lived and looked, the man had seemed normal. The only assumption, and it was weak at best, was that the man was genius level, borderline mad.

'What's the deal with this murder? How many weeks is it now?' Goddard asked from his side of the desk. There had been the handshake on entering, the usual general chat about the weather, the family, the poor state of the economy. Isaac had regarded the man as a friend, still did, and as a mentor. It had been DCS Goddard, then an inspector, who had taken the young Isaac Cook under his wing and had put him into plain clothes and then into Homicide. The two men had a long history where both of their careers had been on the line, where both had felt the wrath of their seniors. At least with this case there was no escalating murder count, no politician attempting to distort the evidence and looking for a cover-up. There had been a few of those in the past, and whereas he, Isaac Cook, remained idealistic, he knew that his senior had sold out.

Not that Isaac could blame him. There had been a time when he had felt that professionalism and competency and delivering results were the way to the top. But now, even more so than before, there was another factor, missing in his case, apparent in Goddard's, and that was licking the boots of those who controlled an officer's ascension in the Met.

It had not been difficult with the previous commissioner, as he had been a decent man. But now Richard Goddard had to get past Alwyn Davies, the new commissioner. Goddard, as much as he tried, was not Davies's type of man, never would be. The problem was that Davies, a man who abhorred sycophants, or at least he said he did, cherished those who stroked him the right way and covered up his shortcomings, and Isaac knew he had a few of those. The general consensus in the police force was that the commissioner had no clue what he was doing, which raised the question of how he had obtained the position in the first place.

There were some that thought it was part of a larger plan to split the Met, form it into smaller units, even privatise it, and the best way to ensure a satisfactory result was to drive it down into oblivion, and Davies was certainly doing a good job at that.

The forces were rallying in the Met. On the one side were those who wanted it to stay the way it was, only with competent leadership, sans Alwyn Davies. Isaac belonged to that group. Others wanted the splitting, the privatisation, but Isaac thought they were motivated by self, not out of any belief that law and order would gain from it, even if it could. The level of lawlessness in society was not looking good. Some areas of the city were under the control of gangs, even around Notting Hill, which sat right in Challis Street Police Station's area of operation. So far their impact had been controllable, but not for much longer if the police force continued to be stripped of its best officers, and other areas of London had been entirely taken over by the gangs, some just hooligans with knives and guns, other with a religious intent, willing to kill at random those that they despised.

Richard Goddard, Isaac knew, sat somewhere in the middle. A decent man who cared about law and order, a man who hoped to be the commissioner one day, and whose plan was being thwarted by the forces of evil, or at least that was how Isaac saw them. How could any right-minded person in the police force want to dilute the most respected police operation in the world, namely the London Metropolitan Police? Even he, Isaac, had considered his options. He should have been a superintendent by now, Goddard a commander, and they had both played the game, but politics had got in the way.

'We've no further information on the murderer,' Isaac said. 'The team's out looking.'

'The case against this man, watertight?' Goddard asked.

'The man admitted to killing him.'

'Will it hold up in a court of law?'

'Probably not if he changes his story, but we've not caught him yet.'

'I give you a simple murder case, one murder, one murderer, and you can't find him. What is it with your department?'

Isaac had been through this rigmarole before: the negativity, the criticism, and eventually the acquiescing and being able to sit down and hold a rational discussion about the Homicide department and its current workload, which was always an oblique way of discussing budgetary concerns, and the latest state of the investigation.

'The case is proceeding well,' Isaac said, although he was not convinced that it was.

'Rubbish. You've no idea where or who this man is. We've known each other for a long time, you can be truthful with me.'

'It's true, the man has disappeared, and there is still the unknown about who he is, what he is. We've checked out the notebook that was with Bob Robertson, and then there is the computer theft at the hostel: both very suspicious.'

64

'Do you think the man was hiding out?'

'It's crossed our minds, but on the street, living in those conditions? If he's educated, the assumption would be that he had some money to live better.'

'Where's a better disguise than on the street?' Goddard said.

'Agreed, but it's a harsh way to conceal yourself. It makes no sense.'

'The man makes no sense. Looking at it logically is not going to solve this case. Have you checked all possible locations where this man could have disappeared?'

'There's one or two to complete. After that, we're not sure where to go.'

'Do you want to put this case on the back burner for a while?'

'Not yet,' Isaac said. 'We're not ready for that yet.'

***

It was strange, Big Greg reflected as he sat in a café not far from where his daughter lived. When he had been a tramp, smelly and dishevelled, his daughter had treated him with kindness, but now, the first time that he had seen her since his transformation, she had been abusive. He knew that he should not have touched the baby in its pushchair, not attempted to give her a sweet to eat, but it had been so many years since he had felt any fondness in his life, and if he could not have it from his wife, then perhaps from his daughter, who had been young when he had left, so much so that she had not recognised him. Back then, he had been fair-haired with it combed to one side and worn long, touching his shoulders. Now he had close-cropped hair with a neatly-trimmed beard.

He had to admit that in the weeks since his return from being homeless to being a viable member of society, his physical condition had changed immeasurably. The old clothes that he had worn, dumped in a bin not far from the hostel where he had completed his transformation, the smell that he had worn, long removed, along with the stains on his teeth. He had needed a couple of fillings as well as some serious hygiene work from a dental hygienist who was none too gentle with her prodding into his gums. He had disliked the regular visits as a child to the dentist; his dislike had not tempered. A three-week strict exercise regime had removed most of the excess weight, although the skin in some areas of his body was still loose, and the daily run had dealt with his breathing. All in all, he had to reflect that considering the years of neglect he had not turned out bad, and still his daughter had told him to go away or she'd call the police.

He had wanted to tell her, desperately so, but he couldn't. Now was not the time; the threat remained. They had used violence before, even threatened to use it against his family.

He had known back then that if he escaped, they would use his wife and daughter, to make him reappear. That was why he had chosen to fake a suicide and to live on the street. It had not been the solution he would have chosen, considering that he had been a fastidious man, always obsessing on his appearance and his cleanliness. He remembered his wife's comments as if it was yesterday: 'You look lovely. Now hurry up, we've got to go,' she would say. How he missed her and her affection. He had had to endure her having him declared legally dead, then watch her falling in love with another man, eventually moving in with him.

He tried to imagine her reaction if he reappeared, a man back from the dead, but then there'd be questions about what had happened to the man whose name and appearance he had affected for so long. He plotted the way forward, knowing that before the end, if he was there at that time, he would reveal himself to his daughter, be allowed for one time to hold his granddaughter, to give her a sweet and a present without the child's mother ripping them away.

Big Greg, now answering to his own name of Malcolm, walked away from the café and headed back to the flat he had leased on a short-term basis. He turned on the television and watched the news. Nothing had changed that he could see; there were still wars, distrust and hate. He knew that if he had given

66

them what they had wanted all those years ago, it could have been worse in that they would have in addition a weapon that he had been instrumental in developing. He considered the options.

It was clear that those who had the computer would not stop; he knew them too well, their avarice, their support from the military.

***

'Remember me?' Malcolm said as he stood at the entrance to the terrace house on Kensington Park Road in Holland Park. He was surprised the man had opened the door considering the nature of the business he was involved in.

'What do you want?' the man replied in a gruff voice. Big Greg looked at him, remembered the last time he had seen him. Back then, he had been tied to a chair, the man in front of him hovering close, threatening to allow another man to inflict pain on his daughter and then his wife.

'Think back.'

'Leave or else.'

'Or else what? You'll call the police?'

'Yes.'

'It'll be too late by then.'

'Why?'

Big Greg, much larger than the man standing in front of him, pushed forward and closed the door behind him.

'You've no right to accost me in my house. Don't you know who I am?'

'I know only too well who you are. A dealer in death, a man sanctioned to extract information, and you don't care who you threaten or torture. I was one of your victims. Most don't live, but I did, knowing that one day I would return and deal with you for what you did to me.'

Chapter 10

Isaac was in his car, preparing to leave Challis Street Police Station. It was eight in the evening. The phone call from Larry Hill caused him to turn right instead of left on leaving the carpark.

'There's a body,' Larry had said.

'Murder?' Isaac's reply.

'It seems that way.'

'I'll be there in ten minutes. Gordon Windsor?'

'I've phoned him.'

A neat white-painted terrace house in Holland Park, just the same as all the others along the street. Isaac knew this part of London; it was where the wealthy lived, where he had seen a few too many murders over the years, and now another one.

Sometimes, when he had the time to consider such matters, he wondered what it was with these people. On the face of it they had all that they wanted, yet they indulged in petty squabbles, occasional violence, the occasional murder, the same as everyone else. At least it was a different street this time, although the procedure was the same: establish the crime scene, keep the onlookers away, put on overalls, gloves, and foot protectors.

After more than once being told by Gordon Windsor, Isaac always made sure he had two sets of protective gear in the back of his car.

'What's the situation here?' Isaac asked the uniform at the door.

'Male, fifty-two, dead.'

'Anything more?'

'Just a name.'

'And?'

'George Arbuthnot.'

'Unusual name,' Isaac replied to the uniform, a young man, new to Challis Street, who obviously was a man of few words. Not that it concerned Isaac. Some were too wordy, and the man had given him the salient facts, would have told him more if he had asked.

'The man's been strangled. It's a messy job,' Larry said.

'What do you mean?'

'He was tied to a chair in the dining room. There are signs of violence before he was garrotted with fencing wire.'

'It sounds unpleasant,' Isaac said as he entered the room, making sure not to impede the crime scene investigators.

'The man's been tortured,' Gordon Windsor said. He had arrived a few minutes before Isaac.

'Any details?'

'Looking at the left hand, I'd say the wrist has been broken.'

'With force?'

'It seems intentional, and then, if you look at the face, you can see where he has repeatedly been hit, signs of broken teeth.'

'Was an implement used?' Larry asked.

The three men stood close to the body. Two of Windsor's team were nearby, checking for fingerprints, taking samples from the blood splattered on the wall. Nobody in that dining room was in the least perturbed by the sight of the dead man and the fact that he had suffered a painful and needlessly violent death. To them, it was academic.

'I'd say a mallet used to tenderise meat was used to smash the man's face, probably used to break the wrist as well.'

'Any ideas as to the murderer?'

'That's the easy one. I can tell you who did this, subject to forensics, that is,' Windsor said.

'Your opinion will suffice,' Isaac said.

'We found a fingerprint on the mallet.'

'And?' Isaac asked, anxious for the man to stop savouring the moment and to give them the answer.

69

'It matches a print we found at Robertson's hostel. Neither print is good enough to run through the Fingerprint's database, though.'

'Big Greg?' Larry said.

'It's more than probable, although, without the man, it's not possible to prove that conclusively.'

Isaac realised that yet again one murder had increased to two. And once that occurred, then there would be more. In this instance, the killing of Arbuthnot was premeditated, as if the man had planned this for some time. It had been assumed with Bob Robertson that the crime had been committed in anger, but there was no way that the body in the chair in front of them, its head angled back, the wire around its neck, was the result of a momentary action. It had the look of a premeditated murder carried out calmly and with care.

'What do we know about the victim?' Isaac asked.

'Not a lot at the present moment,' Larry said. 'He was found by the lady who comes in every other day to tidy up. According to her, he was a man who kept to himself.'

'The housekeeper?' Isaac asked.

'She's in the other room.'

***

A female police constable was with the housekeeper. The two women were sitting on a sofa close to an electric heater, the type that had imitation flames.

'You found the body?' Isaac asked. He and Larry had introduced themselves first, excused the policewoman who had left the room.

'I come here every two days, do my work and leave,' the housekeeper said. It was evident from her accent that she was not English.

'Your name is Lena Szabo?' Isaac asked.

'Yes. I came here ten years ago with my husband from Hungary. We are English citizens now.'

Larry assumed the woman had mentioned that she was English to forestall the inevitable question about whether she was one of the recent immigrants into the country, some of whom were causing trouble.

'Have you worked here long?'

'Two years. I did not know Mr Arbuthnot very well.'

'Why's that?'

'I only saw him once or twice a month. Normally, the house was empty when I came here. I'd do my work and leave.'

'What can you tell us about him?'

'He paid me well. He was polite, nothing more.'

'Any friends, what sort of business he was involved in?'

'Nothing. I did my job and left, that's all.'

'You don't seem upset,' Larry said.

'I've seen death before.'

'When?'

'I was a child in 1956 when the Russians quelled the uprising. I saw the people shot on the street. I saw what happened if the mob got their hands on a member of the secret police.'

'Did you like Mr Arbuthnot?' Isaac asked.

'Not very much.'

'Why?'

'He was a cruel man.'

'Why do you say that?'

'There was a dog next door, always barking. It was poisoned.'

'Do you believe he poisoned it?'

'I saw the poison, or what was left of it, in the bin that I emptied. He did not know that I had seen it.'

'Yet you continued to work for him.'

'Yes.'

'Why?'

'One dog is nothing compared to seeing tens of people, some of them were my age, gunned down as they waited to buy bread. You have seen death, you must understand.'

Isaac could only agree with the woman. The sight of a man with wire around his neck, a decomposed and dismembered corpse, a man fished out of the river after three weeks weighted down. None of them had upset him greatly, none had disturbed his appetite or his nights out. He had to concede the woman's disinterest in the dead body.

***

With Big Greg almost certainly back in the area, Isaac told Katrina Ireland to be on the lookout.

The man was now regarded as violent, likely to kill again, but so far they had no motive. Bob Robertson ran a hostel for the disadvantaged, George Arbuthnot, it was found out, was a retired civil servant. No connection could be established between the two men.

Robertson was known to be a compassionate man; Arbuthnot was not if the dog poisoning story was true, and there was no reason to doubt the housekeeper's statement. Bridget, as per the standard procedure, had checked out Lena Szabo's story, and it was found to be correct. She and her husband had entered England ten years previously, worked hard, been granted citizenship, and were respected members of the community.

George Arbuthnot, however, remained a mystery. Bridget had conducted the usual checks: age, background, financial status, employment. What they had shown was that the man had been a middle-ranking civil servant, yet he lived in a house, with a clear title in his name, that would have been way out of his pay scale.

'Bridget, what do we know about Arbuthnot, apart from the usual?' Isaac asked. The last few weeks of regular hours were gone. Wendy knew it would be back to the early morning meetings where the core team would meet in the DCI's office to discuss the way forward.

Larry Hill knew that his wife's macrobiotic diets and the meals she prepared for him every day in plastic containers would not suffice; he'd be sneaking in the extra meal here and there to survive the day. An early morning English breakfast, heavy on the stomach, good for energy, would see him through, and no doubt a few drinks in the pub to loosen the tongues of anyone willing to talk. Isaac knew it would be affecting his love life again, which he regretted to some extent, but not as much as he thought it should. And as for Bridget, she'd have the office computer, the files to prepare, the spreadsheets to set up; to her that was heaven. She knew she'd be in the office bright and early, leaving late. Isaac knew, as he always did, that none of them would let him down.

'I've set up an all points for the man,' Larry said.

'There's only one problem,' Wendy said.

'What's that?' Isaac asked.

'I'd organised a door-to-door in the area of Arbuthnot's house. We know the approximate times when Big Greg entered the house and when he left, within a few hours either way.'

'What were the results?'

'We've a few more streets to conclude today, but one thing is clear. No vagrant or homeless person knocked on Arbuthnot's door.'

'Conclusive?' Isaac asked.

'Ninety per cent, I'd say. Some high-fliers live down there, some politicians. As a result, the security in the area is tight. Apart from the police keeping a watch on the area, some of the occupants have contracted local security firms to keep roving twenty-four-hour patrols in the area. Anyone fitting the description of Big Greg would not have got within one hundred yards of Arbuthnot's house.'

'What does that mean?' Larry asked.

'The man is no longer dressed the way he was,' Wendy replied.

'Which means?'

'It's fairly obvious. The homeless act was just that. He's now back dressed as you and I.'

'But why?' Isaac asked. 'It makes no sense, none of it.'

'That doesn't matter, does it, guv?' Wendy said. 'What's important is that he's back, he's murdering people for a reason, and he'll not stop.'

'Not again,' Isaac said. He could see Goddard and then the commissioner on the warpath again. He wished he was back on holiday in Jamaica.

'Any idea what the man looks like now?' Larry asked.

'We're checking. It's possible we'll be able to come up with something,' Wendy said.

'Work with Bridget on this. It's our priority now,' Isaac said.

'And you, guv?'

'I'll need to tell our senior. It's better for him to hear it from me than Commissioner Davies.'

'How will he know?' Bridget asked.

'He's got someone in Challis Street keeping him updated.'

'Do you know who?'

'Not yet.'

***

Big Greg had not enjoyed torturing Arbuthnot, but he had done what was necessary. The man had secrets that needed to be revealed. It had surprised him how easy it had been.

In the past, when he had been on the receiving end of Arbuthnot and the other man's skills, he had endured for days, but then he had a reason to keep quiet, a reason to take the pain, but what did his torturer have, apart from a depressingly affluent house?

Big Greg reflected on his house from all those years before. How there would always be a flower in a vase, a crayon drawing of his daughter's held onto the fridge door with a magnet. And how his daughter would fling her arms around his neck when he came in after work, and he'd swing her around, being chastised by the mother for getting the girl excited just before her bedtime.

Happy memories of a reality long gone, and now it had all been replaced by anger and hatred and the need to inflict pain and suffering on those who had forced him to live a life of disgust and loathing. Arbuthnot had been the first, he would not be the last.

He wondered if the years and the anguish were driving him mad, but he knew they were not. He could see it all so clearly: the need to retrieve all of his notes from where they were stored, not to allow anyone to get in his way. And then he had to let his daughter know that her father still loved her and that he would protect her.

He had to admit that he enjoyed being back again, and the small flat that he had rented was adequate for his purposes. The laptop with its Wi-Fi was keeping him up to date on the current situation, especially those who needed to be dealt with. It was unfortunate that some, those he had worked with, were innocent of any guilt other than they may find the solution.

The others, who had set up the research team, convincing in their argument that their results would only be used for peaceful purposes, yet knowing full well that its funding was military, deserved special treatment.

But even if he completed his task, would it be sufficient to ensure that no one would attempt to solve the technical problems, whether in England or overseas? People were becoming more educated, and computers more capable of processing the millions of computations that would be required, and there was no way the military in his country or any other would ever acquiesce to his request to leave well alone.

It had been only eleven years on the street, yet when he looked in the mirror he saw an old man. He looked at the picture of himself that he had carried in that old coat for so many years: a photo of him with his wife and daughter. Then he had been a young man, fit and robust with a healthy tan, but now his skin was weakened, his features not so well defined. He knew that if he stood in front of his wife, she would not instantly recognise him, nor would her husband, one of those that he needed to kill.

For her sake, he did not want to, but there were more important considerations.

Big Greg decided that his wife's husband would be next. He took a beer from the fridge, a luxury he had denied himself on the street. He opened the bottle and took a swig, the first of many that night. He turned on the television; a mind-numbing movie of no great worth, but for once, nonsense was better than the reality. For that evening, he would forget.

Chapter 11

Wendy had finally had some success. For a police officer with a formidable reputation inside Challis Street Police Station, as well as in the other stations in the area, her inability to trace Big Greg had been an embarrassment to her.

Isaac had told her to keep looking and to ignore the occasionally barbed jibe in her direction, as Isaac knew they were obliquely directed at him. The eloquent black man was the bane of one or two of the older inhabitants of the police station who still harboured attitudes not in line with society in general. Isaac had learnt to deal with them, but now there was some deflection onto those who supported him. No doubt admirers of Commissioner Davies, he assumed, a man who did not conceal his dislikes too well, and a man anxious to get DCI Caddick back into Challis Street. The last Isaac had heard of the man he was assigned to a regional police station to the north of London and generally upsetting those he worked for, as well as producing limited results. But somehow Caddick continued to prosper, and the last word was that he was likely to make superintendent within the next six months, a clear sign that friends in high places were always beneficial.

Isaac assumed it was the result of sucking up to seniors you neither liked nor respected. He was glad he didn't have to do it. If he didn't like someone, he was not good at pretending, but Goddard was, although the results were not good for him. The man had been passed over for the rank of commander on more than one occasion; the usual reasons given were budgets, experience, age.

Politics did not only have a place in the Houses of Parliament; they were also alive and well in the Met, an august organisation that prided itself on its fair-mindedness, its willingness to bring in all colours, all religions, all genders, even those who were openly gay. Not that Isaac minded, as he had prospered due to the political correctness, but he had noticed the percentages of those being promoted who were deemed not to be Anglo-Saxon and white had slipped under Davies's watch. It was only fractional, but Isaac kept a watch on such issues, knowing full well that if Davies were not there, then Goddard would take the next rung up the ladder towards commissioner, and he, Isaac Cook, would almost certainly make superintendent, then commander, and ultimately commissioner.

It was only four years previously that he had been shown on publicity promotions to join the modern police force. There he had been, his beaming face proudly proclaiming that the Met embraced all people and that he was committed to the organisation, yet now he sometimes felt that he did not belong. Still, he had no intention of complaining, and there was a murder investigation to conclude.

'What have you found?' Isaac asked. It was early afternoon, and the team were in the office. Typically, Isaac would have expected everyone to be out or working in the office on related activities, but Wendy had been adamant that they should get together.

'I've found where Big Greg went to after leaving Katrina Ireland.' Isaac could see that Wendy was pleased with herself when she announced the news.

'How?' Larry asked. He'd been looking, as well as checking into George Arbuthnot's background. Yet again, it had been Wendy who had made the breakthrough.

'I just kept widening the search area. It's further away than I thought.'

'Where and what did you find out?' Isaac asked. Wendy had had her moment of glory, now they needed the details.

'He checked into a hostel in Croydon. It's definitely him, as the description fits, and the person in charge recognised him from some years before. It seems that our man is unmistakable, but then we already knew that.'

'Then what?'

'Big Greg checked in, but he never checked out.'

'What do you mean?' Larry asked.

'He went up to the first floor of the building. He was carrying a small case with him. He showered, supposedly used all the hot water, and left wearing different clothes.'

'Clothes from the case?' Isaac asked.

'No one saw him leave.'

'If no one saw him leave, then how do you know he changed his clothes?'

'He dumped the old clothes he had been wearing into a bin outside, that's how.'

'Do we have a new description for the man?'

'I'm working on that. But for now, we're not looking for a tramp.'

'Almost impossible to find, apart from the unkempt hair and beard.'

'There's a barber's shop not far from the hostel,' Wendy said.

'He's cut it off?'

'The only reason the man remembered was the condition of the hair and beard. He didn't give me much other than he had trimmed the beard, cut the hair very short.'

'Clothing? Did the man give you a description?'

'No. He just remembered the hair, that's all.'

'And the case?' Isaac asked.

'He left it at the hostel. It wasn't there when I got there, but that's not surprising. Anyone could have taken it.'

'Our all points warning is no longer relevant, is it?'

'No, but it helps with finding out who visited George Arbuthnot.'

***

Two men met. One of them was in his late forties and dressed in a suit, the other man, older but still fit, lounged in a chair. Neither of the two men liked the other, but that was not important. What was important was the death of George Arbuthnot, and its significance.

'He's back,' the suited man said.

'We always assumed he was dead.' The lounging man raised himself from his chair. It was late at night, and they did not meet often. He was holding a beer in one hand.

'I always believed that he had faked his death.'

'What do you mean? Are you telling me that you have always regarded his death as suspicious?'

'There was never any body.'

'All the evidence pointed to his death.'

'The man held out against Arbuthnot and then managed to escape. It's hardly the behaviour of someone about to commit suicide.'

'And now that Arbuthnot's dead, you're assuming it's him?'

'Why not? The man may have been brilliant, but he was borderline psychotic. Genius level intellect bordering on madness. He'd not be the first one to flip.'

'I'll grant you that Arbuthnot's death was violent, but why let us know that he's back? He must have realised that we'd go looking for him.'

'Maybe he has, or maybe he's not thought it through.'

'Whatever happens, we need to draw him out.'

'His family?'

'Go for the daughter. He was always fond of her.'

***

Big Greg walked past the place where he had worked. He wore a baseball cap, and he had pulled up the collar of his jacket. He had seen those who concerned him, but he knew that they were only the minor functionaries. There were others more senior that concerned him more.

Others who had given the order for him to be detained and for the truth to be extracted at all costs. A smart man, he knew that what he had started he had to conclude. Until then, nobody was safe. He reconsidered his position, took stock of his current financial status, and the time he'd allotted to complete his plan.

He knew that he was endangering his family and that they must be protected at all times. His analytical brain could see the pros and cons, the percentage for and against a particular action. Arbuthnot's death would have raised an alarm, although they would not be certain that it was him.

Hadn't he covered his tracks well, ensured that his death was indisputable? In the eleven years that he had remained hidden, his family had not been harmed, and now he had to kill his wife's lover. He did not want to do it, knew that he had to.

In the meantime, there were others that needed to be dealt with. All the links to what he had discovered had to be severed, all possibility of anyone finding the solution to his research. Only then would it be safe, only then could he discard his clothes and walk out into the cold sea. He knew that once all the loose ends had been dealt with, he would have to die. There was always another one like Arbuthnot who would not hesitate to subject him to pain, to force him to give them the knowledge he had in his mind. And there were others in government and the military who would not hesitate to give the order, men who remained nameless, hidden behind doors, not wanting to be confronted with the reality of extraction, only the result.

Big Greg remembered the military men who had spoken to the research director. First, he had to protect his family, but how would he contact them? Would they listen to a man from the past? Would his daughter understand, or would his wife realise that the truth of the man she now loved was that he was no more than a charlatan and he deserved to die?

The thoughts bubbled through the man's mind as he weighed up the situation, knowing full well that the burden placed on him was too much.

Big Greg found a café and ordered a café latte. He entered a phone number into the mobile phone that he had purchased. It was nothing special, not a smartphone, but it could make calls, even receive them, but no one had his number. The phone was answered, a woman's voice could be heard. 'Gwen Barrow.'

At the sound of the voice, a voice he had not heard for a long time, Big Greg hung up. *She's taken his name*, he thought. *The name of the man that I must kill.*

He sat there silently for several minutes, recollecting when they had first met, he and Gwen. They had both been young and idealistic. He was fresh out of university, she was already forging a career as an accountant. They had been happy years, enhanced by the arrival of their daughter, a cheerful, cherubic little girl with a lovely smile, even as a baby.

They had loved the child equally, but he was always her favourite, not that it worried Gwen. He still loved Gwen, he knew that, even if he could not bear to hear her voice again, knowing that another man had loved her after him.

He had seen the anguish, the sorrow on her face after he had drowned, although no body had ever been found. He had been pleased, at least for his wife, that after two years of mourning she had started to enjoy life again, and Ed Barrow had been a good father to his daughter, a loving husband to his wife.

Ed had been a colleague, and he had thought him to be a good man, but then he had seen him with the military men.

Big Greg wondered why he had waited so long to act. His wife's husband, his daughter's stepfather, was one of those responsible for the treatment that had been meted out to him, the reason that he had vanished for so many years, the reason why he now plotted Barrow's death.

He needed to explain to Gwen, he knew that, but how would he tell her? Would she believe him or would she believe the man that she had married, the man that she apparently loved, but it could not be the way she had loved him. At least, he hoped it wasn't, but they always seemed to be comfortable in each other's presence. And as for his daughter, she had accepted the man who had married her mother, the man who had allowed her father to be tortured, the man who had sold out their research for the betterment of mankind to the military, knowing that they would use it for violence.

How would his wife deal with that realisation? Would his daughter be capable of understanding? He knew they would not.

Big Greg moved on, his destination unclear. Again he walked past the building where he had worked. He peered through the glass pane of the front door. Inside nothing had changed. There was the man at the desk checking passes, giving the courtesy 'good morning', 'good afternoon', 'see you tomorrow'. The urge to enter through the door was irresistible. He pushed against it, it opened, and he walked inside. He still wore the baseball cap and the jacket with the upturned collar. He took out a pair of prescription glasses to complete the disguise that had been in their case. He put them on; they were too weak, and the man at the desk was a blur.

'Can I help you, sir?' the man asked. Big Greg recognised the voice. It was the same man who had worked there all those years previously.

'No thanks. I think I've entered the wrong building.' Big Greg left. The man had not recognised him, maybe his wife wouldn't, maybe Ed Barrow wouldn't either.

Chapter 12

Larry Hill had to admit that the day had started well. It was still early, and there was a full-scale murder enquiry in place, the chance to indulge in an English breakfast at his favourite café in Notting Hill. He knew his wife would be upset, but he wouldn't be home before ten that evening.

The waitress had not needed to ask for his order; she knew what he wanted, it was always the same: two eggs, the same number of sausages, some bacon and toast, and freshly-brewed coffee to wash it down. 'Busy day?' she asked.

'The usual,' Larry's reply.

'Another murder?'

'What else.'

'Don't you ever get upset with seeing dead bodies?' the waitress asked. Larry remembered how she had looked when he had told her about the dismembered corpse they'd fished out of the canal in a previous case. No doubt she would be able to manage his description of Arbuthnot with wire tight around his neck better than his description of a headless body, but he did not intend to find out.

'You get used to it,' he said instead.

After he had finished his breakfast, and he had drunk his third cup of coffee, he left the café and headed over to Arbuthnot's house. A uniform stood outside, the crime scene tape across the door. Larry showed his identification, a formality as the two men knew each other.

Gordon Windsor and his team had been over the house, and apart from the room where the murder had occurred, there was no other evidence apart from signs of a struggle in the hall. Larry put gloves on. He climbed the stairs to the first floor of the terrace house, unsure of what he was looking for, other than some insight into who the man had been.

All they had found out so far was that the man had been a middle-ranking civil servant, that he had travelled a lot, and he appeared to have had no defined place of work. Isaac thought that he may have been MI5 or MI6, although that had been discounted for the present.

DCS Goddard had used his contacts; Isaac assumed it was Angus McTavish, the former government whip, now a lord, who had checked it out. If that was the case, then McTavish and the truth were not always mutually compatible, although in this case Isaac had been willing to give the man the benefit of the doubt.

But that was only because they did not know why Arbuthnot had been killed and who Big Greg was. Wendy was working on finding out more about Big Greg, as was Bridget on her computer, although Larry thought that Arbuthnot was the key.

And why was Big Greg now visible, no longer a vagrant? He'd even been spotted by one of Arbuthnot's neighbours according to a second door-to-door with the updated description of the man. Not that it helped much, as the man at Arbuthnot's door had been tall, erect, with short hair. Apart from the tall, there wasn't much to go on, no more than the barber in Croydon had been able to give.

Regardless, Larry was in the house methodically checking from room to room. He could have brought someone else with him, but Wendy was busy and the others in the department would have needed him to hold their hands, and he needed to focus. His wife phoned. 'How's the snack I prepared for you?' she asked.

Larry felt some guilt, remembered the sad-looking piece of lettuce with tomato slices. 'Great, thanks.'

'Good, and don't you go eating the wrong kinds of food, and no drinking beer. Tonight's special, you know that.'

It was their wedding anniversary. He had forgotten, and now he had a murder case, a full breakfast, and a strong possibility that he would be phoning his wife again before the day was out, profusely apologising, knowing full well the reaction on the other end of the phone line. 'See you later,' he said.

His wife hung up; he went back to checking the house. The first floor revealed nothing of interest, only two bedrooms and a small study that the man had used for storing his golf clubs, a few empty suitcases.

He ascended the second flight of stairs and entered the main bedroom. Larry thought the man's choice of decor was strange. Apart from a double bed in the centre of the room, there was not much else except for a zebra skin on the wall, one or two pictures of men in military uniform, although they looked old, and a table on one side of the bed. He opened the drawer of the table. Inside were a photo album, a mobile phone, and a list of names on a piece of paper. Larry took a picture of the items in situ. He then removed them and placed them in evidence bags. He'd get Bridget to check through them at Challis Street.

He looked into another room adjoining the main bedroom. He found the man's passport, a magnetic ID card, and a bank statement. He briefly looked at the balance on the statement, let out a sigh when he saw the zeros at the end of the total amount.

***

Gwen Barrow had not expected to receive a phone call. She had heard the man's breathing on the other end. There had been phone calls in the past when no one had spoken, but that was a long time ago, long before she had moved in with Ed. Since then, her life had stabilised, and she could admit to being happy, although the doubt over her first husband always lingered.

He had indicated on a couple of occasions that his work was at a critical stage and that he was not sure what to do. She had asked him, even once after they had downed a good bottle of red together, but he had not wanted to say more. 'It's best if you don't know,' he had said.

Gwen did not know why the phone call had reminded her of her dead husband, but it had. She shivered at the thought of it, as if a ghost had arisen.

She looked at the number on her phone; it meant nothing to her. She dialled it: busy tone. She did not know why she did not mention it to Ed when he came in later.

The death of her first husband had troubled her for a long time after the police officer had stood at the door to inform her of his disappearance. She remembered that Ed was the first one from the department where he had worked who had come over to offer his condolences. It was ironic that the two men, her two husbands, had been such great friends. One was academic and intense, the other an able administrator, although not with the same intellect, and one was dead, the other very much alive.

It was strange, she thought, how life turns out. Her daughter had struggled at school for many years, had drifted into alcohol and recreational drugs and bad men, but now she was married and sensible, holding down a good job. Malcolm's death had come as a great shock to both mother and daughter, and that it had been suicide when there had been no reason.

He had phoned her two hours before to tell her that he loved her, always would, and that he would be keeping a watch out for her and their daughter. And then he was gone, apart from a suicide note she received in the mail.

Ed had been there from the start, although it was sometime before they became lovers, and then husband and wife. He had proven himself to be a good substitute father in accepting her child with Malcolm, so much so that Ed had walked her daughter down the aisle when she had married.

And now a phone call, the breathing on the other end so recognisable, yet impossible. She pushed the thought to the back of her mind, realised that it was fanciful make-believe. Anyway, she had Ed.

***

Two constants remained in Big Greg's mind: love and hate. He knew that the hatred for others could not be allowed to destroy the love he felt for his wife and his daughter. But he was aware that the path he was inexorably marching down would threaten that love, possibly exclude some of those he hated.

Big Greg wondered if Ed's marriage to Gwen had been a way for him to keep watch on her, not believing that he had walked out into that cold sea and drowned. It had seemed possible that his fears about Ed had been true at first, but now he could see the affection in the man for the two people that he cared about most in the world. They were within touching distance and he could not touch.

It troubled him greatly. In all the years since he had been declared missing, presumed dead, he had not felt the warmth of a woman alongside him. Now with his fitness regained, he felt the need. He considered an escort; there were plenty available, even the woman at the hostel had been one, he knew. He had seen her accosting men on the street, her dress slit high on one side, her breasts protruding out of her top. Her transformation into a decent citizen had been remarkable, almost as good as his, but she had not murdered anyone; she was free to come and go as she pleased, whereas he had to hide in the shadows.

Not that he begrudged her. After all, he could have just given them the solution that they wanted, that Ed had wanted, that Arbuthnot and his torturing partner had attempted to extract from him, but he had made his decision, chosen which bed to lie on.

Big Greg turned away from the entrance to the park where his daughter was gently pushing his granddaughter in a swing. Today was not the day to reveal himself; today was a day for action.

***

Larry, back in the office, conscious of his wedding anniversary, sat with Bridget. The two were looking through the evidence that he had brought back from Arbuthnot's bedroom. The photo album, only small, no more than fifty photos, most of his travels, was not of much interest, save for three photos with four people in each, including Arbuthnot.

'The sort of photos you'd take at a department's Christmas party,' Bridget said. Larry could see what she meant.

'Unusual,' Larry said. 'Most people take those photos, never look at them again, and, nowadays they're stored on a smartphone, not in an album.'

The passport revealed that the man had travelled extensively, sometimes to countries off the beaten track, but there was nothing suspicious in that. Bridget had discovered, as had Isaac through Goddard's contact, that the man was a facilitator, putting together deals with foreign governments that were not by their nature illegal, but would be regarded as dubious.

Larry thought it must be something to do with weapons sales, which made sense, in that the British Government, or any government, is not averse to selling weapons, although some of those purchasing them could be less than democratic, more likely to shoot their own people or attack the neighbouring country, even give the weapons to terrorists.

Whatever it was, George Arbuthnot was not a middle-ranking civil servant. Bridget had checked the man's bank statement, and found it to be genuine.

The photos continued to be of interest. Bridget had taken enhanced photos of each of the individuals and was attempting to match them with the police database. Not that she held out much hope for success as the people in the photos, four men and three women in total, showed no distinguishing features.

Putting the photos to one side, Bridget checked the phone numbers on Arbuthnot's mobile phone; most were of no interest, although some were clearly government.

Larry called some of them to see if he could find out whose they were. It was assumed that most would be unlisted, especially if, as suspected, Arbuthnot was involved in the selling of weapons.

Larry left Bridget and went to speak with Isaac; the man was deep in thought when he entered. 'What is it, guv?'

'The usual.'

'DCS Goddard.'

'You've got it. Arbuthnot's death is causing waves.'

'Waves? What do you mean?'

'The sort of waves that tell us Arbuthnot was more important than he appeared to be.'

'We know that already.'

'The man's passport?'

'I reckon he was up to no good for the British arms industry.'

'That's what Goddard inferred, although I've no idea what it all means, and his murderer, who the hell is he?'

'Whoever he is, he's out there, and he would not have killed without reason.'

'Anything more on him?' Isaac asked. Larry could see that Goddard, and by inference Commissioner Alwyn Davies, was placing special emphasis on the Challis Street Homicide department, and yet again the British Government was involved.

'Wendy's trying, but the man disappears. We have an approximate idea of what he looks like. We've issued an APW on him, but, apart from his height, he'll blend in easily enough, and if he has any experience, if he's involved with Arbuthnot, maybe the same line of business, he'll be able to stay concealed.'

'What about the formulas and the technical drawings in the notebook? Anything more?'

'Bridget's tried, but no.'

'Why did he kill Bob Robertson? That's the one question that confuses me,' Isaac said. 'The man's remained hidden, hiding out as a tramp, sleeping under bridges, eating at charitable hostels when he could, and then he kills a man for no apparent reason, and then he cleans himself up and goes on a killing spree.'

'It's hardly a spree,' Larry said.

'It is, and you know it. Once they start, these sorts of people don't stop. There'll be more murders.'

'Serial killer?'

'Not this man. He's methodical, and he's working to a plan. Arbuthnot's death was not random; the man was tied to him, I'm sure of it, but how do we find out who else was involved?'

'Your political connections, MI5, MI6?'

'I've no intention of trusting McTavish again.'

'You still believe he was implicated in the deaths in a previous case?'

'He was involved. Always made out he wasn't, and now he's sitting in the House of Lords. If I contacted him, he'd give me answers, but I've no idea if they'd be the right answers, not even sure if it would help.'

'We're floundering here. We need a breakthrough from somewhere,' Larry said.

Isaac knew that his DI was correct. Unless the connections were made, then the chances of finding Big Greg were slim. He wondered what sort of man could conceal himself by living on the street, given that the man recited poetry, wrote complicated formulas in notebooks, and killed civil servants who appeared to be involved in arms trading.

Isaac knew that it was going to become more involved as they peeled away the layers, and almost certainly more dangerous. If men such as Bob Robertson could be killed to maintain a secret, if Arbuthnot could be killed, probably for revenge, then how far would Big Greg go? Would he consider a police officer expendable if he started to get below the first few layers that concealed the truth? Isaac knew he had not become a detective chief inspector out of some false naivety. He knew that the man would kill as necessary, whatever the reason.

Chapter 13

The office had a commanding view of the city, an imported desk and a high-backed leather chair. It was a suitable office for Ed Barrow, the director of the research department and the husband of Big Greg's former wife, or as the two men in the room knew him, Malcolm Woolston.

'Why after all these years?' Barrow said to the man sitting opposite.

'Are we certain?'

'It's him, no question.'

'Have you told your wife?' the man opposite said. The two men knew who they were referring to. One was his friend who had consoled his wife after he had died, the other man, older and wiser, had realised the importance of the work he had been doing, ensured that the funding, secretive, well hidden, and government, was available as required. Neither of the two men in the office trusted the other, although it did not matter. With Woolston back, both their livelihoods, their reputations, their lives were at stake.

'I hope it never gets to that stage,' Barrow replied.

'He's marked for death?'

'We need his knowledge first.'

'If he gets away again, you know what he could do?'

'No more than he could do now. The risk remains the same.'

'On your head, you know that.'

'I know it,' Barrow replied.

'It's complicated in that you married his wife.'

'That was unforeseen.'

'It'll be personal with him.'

'The man was dead. I married his widow. What's the problem?'

'If she ever finds out that you never believed him to be dead.'

'She never will. Not from me. Will you tell her?' Barrow said.

'If he's standing in front of me, gun in hand, what do you think?'

'You'll cry like a baby, tell him whatever he wants to hear, do whatever he wants.'

'Of course I will.'

'And afterwards?'

'Once I have the upper hand, I'll kill him without hesitation.'

'Is that what Arbuthnot would have done?'

'The man was a savage. You were there when he and that other man went to work on him. You saw how they held Woolston down, pummelled his face to a pulp, applied electric shocks, threatened his family.'

'Malcolm is a tough bastard. He'll protect them at all costs.'

'He'll come for them if they're threatened again.'

'You'd use them as bait?'

'If they're threatened, he'll give himself up. Is that why you married his wife?'

'Not totally.'

'Barrow, you're a bastard.'

A smile crept across Barrow's face. He knew that he loved his wife, Gwen, even her daughter, but the stakes were bigger than either of them. He knew how to get Malcolm Woolston to give himself up, and this time the man would not be able to get free.

***

Big Greg realised that he should have dealt before with those who had caused him to adopt a life of the destitute, but it had been Robertson who had been the catalyst to cause him to return.

All those years of being careful, and then, in one instance, Robertson had revealed that he, Big Greg, was still alive. There was no way that they would have missed the alert. For once, there was indisputable proof that he was still alive, although he always suspected that they thought that he was. After all, hadn't he phoned his wife to tell her that he'd be looking out for her the same day as he had disappeared. Ed Barrow must have read the signal, even if Gwen had not, and now the man was sitting at his table, sleeping with his wife.

Barrow should be the first, but he could wait. Big Greg had to make sure that his family were safe. He needed to let them know that he was alive, and they should disappear for a while. Only then could he act. But he knew that would not be possible. His daughter would not leave her husband without wanting to tell him, and emotionally how would she handle the knowledge that the father she had mourned, and in whose memory she still placed flowers on a plaque in the local cemetery every Sunday, was still alive. He could only imagine her reaction if he knocked on her door and announced himself.

It was clear that he would not be able to spirit them away, and where would they go? His funds were limited, it would be difficult to conceal them, and there was no way that they could become part of the homeless, not his daughter with a child. The options were few, and he was worried. A can of worms had been opened, and it was not going to close until all the worms were dead.

Big Greg had seen the man that he needed to visit next, leaving Ed Barrow's office. He phoned Ed Barrow. 'Leave them alone,' he said when Barrow answered the phone.

'Malcolm, where are you?' Barrow replied. 'My office door is always open.'

'Not a chance. I'm giving you fair warning. If you harm my family, then you're next.'

'Look here, Malcolm, you stay hidden for all these years, and then you come back and start ordering me around. What right do you have?'

'I have all the right. I knew what you were planning. How you intended to steal what I was developing and then to sell it to the highest bidder.'

'No such thing.'

'Arbuthnot talked. He was my proof. I have it on record.'

'And what are you going to do with it? Tell the press, inform the prime minister. Get real, nobody's interested in a few ratbag countries.'

'You know that's nonsense. It could give England a great financial benefit, a chance for low-cost energy, only you want to use it to make weapons of war.'

'That's how the world works. You may have your idealistic views, but this is the real world, and who do you think is funding us?'

'The military?'

'And where do they get their money?'

'Your people didn't come up with the solution after all these years?'

'You knew they never would, and besides, where are you? Where were you?'

'I was around.'

'I never believed that phoney story about you drowning.'

'Yet you married Gwen.'

'Why not? She's a lovely woman; she could have still been your wife if you hadn't had one of your psychotic episodes.'

'They were not psychotic, they were real.'

'Malcolm, real enough to you, but none of it happened. Arbuthnot may have been a bastard dealing in military weapons, but he was a government employee, and he did not deserve to die.'

Big Greg realised there was some truth in what Barrow said. He had had the occasional episodes of madness, enough to have been confined to a mental institution for short periods where they had sedated him and fed him pills, and subjected him to lengthy discussions with psychoanalysts. But that had been before, and during his homeless period, he had not felt the need to talk to anyone, and the dreams that had plagued him had been strangely absent.

'You talk well, Ed, but I can't trust you. Once I'm up there in your office, you'll have me locked up in a padded cell.'

'Not me, Malcolm. Think about it, remember the past.'

'I saw you with Hutton.'

'The old man?' Ed enquired, jumping up from his seat to look out of the window, trying to catch sight of a man who had once been his friend.

'You'll not see me. I see you're still wearing a suit to work.'

Ed Barrow reacted with alarm; he pressed another button on his desk. A woman came running in, Barrow told her to be quiet. 'Malcolm Woolston,' he mouthed, pointing to the phone in his hand.

'Tell Sue Christie not to bother. You'll not find me.'

'Where the hell are you?' Barrow asked.

'I'm not far. I can see you well enough. Are you still screwing Sue?'

Barrow moved to the window of his office, looked out at the buildings nearby. The sun was reflecting off their windows. It was impossible to distinguish who was looking back.

'I'm smarter than that, you should know that.'

'What is it? A camera?'

'Nothing complicated. Just an internet connection and Skype. I could be outside your door, or a hundred miles away, and you'll never know.'

'Malcolm, this is ridiculous. You need professional help,' Barrow said. He had closed the blinds in his office. Sue Christie was sitting across from him, listening in on the conversation. She was worried.

'I have a list,' Big Greg said. 'If any harm comes to my family, then I will kill you, Ed.'

'No harm will come to them. You have my word.'

'The word of a liar. What use is that? Tell Sue not to take out any life insurance. She has no protection.' The phone line went dead.

'You should have killed him when you had the chance,' Sue Christie said.

'How was I to know that he was going to come back from the dead?' Barrow replied.

'You always knew he was alive. You could have found him.'

'How? The man's been watching this office, and we've no idea where he is. Find that camera he's using.'

'Look at your laptop,' Sue said.

'Hell, the camera's on.'

'The man was always smarter than any of us, you know that. He's probably accessed your files as well.'

Barrow looked down at his laptop, a cartoon face looked back at him. It spoke. 'Remember what I told you. Any harm to my family and you're the first.'

Barrow slammed shut the lid of his laptop. 'We've got the best hacking protection. How did he do that?'

'The same way he'll kill any of us if we touch his family, your family.'

***

Big Greg, after his conversation with Ed Barrow, sat in the park opposite his daughter's place. He knew that at two-thirty in the afternoon she would enter the park by the far gate. His daughter, he knew, was a methodical person, the same as him. It had been how he had dealt with eleven years on the street: one day at a time, the same place for a meal, the same repartee, the same place to bed down.

He knew that Barrow had been correct. He could have just given them what they wanted and gone home to his family. They had intended to use his work for evil, to sell it to the highest bidder, good or bad. He had researched the subject, read up on the wars in the Middle East. Where did they get the weapons that were fired at the English, the Americans, the Russians sometimes? They all came from those countries, sold in some arms deal only to be used against the seller in return.

He was not going to be a party to that, whatever the cost. Hadn't his parents died on holiday in Egypt when visiting the Middle East twenty years previously, and what had it been: an English-made missile launched at a police station that hit them as they were catching the bus to the pyramids. He had vowed then that he would do everything in his power to prevent such an occurrence happening again, and now his family was threatened. He knew Ed Barrow, he knew Sue Christie, and he certainly knew the old man, Harold Hutton. He'd been there, standing in the shadows with Ed Barrow, when he was being tortured by Arbuthnot and the other man, the man he had killed in his escape.

He would deal with Hutton to reinforce what he had said to Barrow.

Across the park, Big Greg could see his daughter. She was playing with her child. Little did she know that a man who was plainly in her vision if she only looked his way was protecting her.

Big Greg stood up from the bench he had been sitting on, quickly read the plaque attached to it: *Dedicated to Mary, by her loving husband Michael*. He felt sad on reading the remembrance of a man for his wife, knowing that he would never have that luxury. He was aware that the road ahead was rocky and would be strewn with casualties. He just needed to ensure that they were the ones he chose.

Chapter 14

There were days when Isaac Cook wondered if it was worth it. His team were working at full stretch, following all the procedures, and still receiving criticism about what they were doing, or at least, what he was doing.

He knew he was working hard, although there were three murders unresolved and one murderer still at large. It was as if Big Greg was playing them for fools. Wendy was now confident that his first name was Malcolm, after another homeless man had told her that he had once said that was his name. The board in the Homicide department now had a picture of Malcolm pinned up alongside a description of Big Greg, as well as a grainy photo that had been taken from a CCTV camera close to Arbuthnot's house. Not that the picture had helped much, as the man's face was not visible, concealed as it was under a baseball cap.

And to top it off, Commissioner Davies was paying a visit to Challis Street. That was not unusual in itself, as the man made a point of visiting one or two of his stations every month, but Isaac knew that it was not purely social, an attempt at rallying the troops or boosting morale – although that was pretty low in Homicide at the present time.

There had been another murder, this time Harold Hutton, a man well known in government circles, an advocate for scientific research. His throat had been cut. When the news had come through, Isaac realised that there'd be hell to pay.

Larry had been first on the scene after Hutton's wife had found the body. Gordon Windsor had quickly identified the cause of death, or at least the implement, a razor-sharp knife, the sort that can be purchased in any high-quality kitchen shop.

'Violent,' Gordon Windsor's only comment as he knelt close to the body. A pool of blood was settling on the floor, the gash in the man's neck visible, a clear sign that his head had been yanked back to intensify his distress as his life oozed from him.

Wendy had been in the office when the phone call came through. She was out at the crime scene no more than five minutes after Larry. She took one look at the body and retreated. 'The murderer?' she asked Larry when he came out ten minutes later.

'Our friend.'

'Conclusive?'

'Windsor will confirm, but it looks to be him.'

'The super's going to be peeved with this. The man was a member of parliament.'

'Have you phoned DCI Cook?'

'He knows,' Wendy replied.

'Not the best day for this to happen, is it?'

'I can't see how our DCI can head Commissioner Davies off on this one. That's three murders now, and we're no closer to solving the case.'

'Hutton had cameras in the house. We're checking now.'

'Would Big Greg have known that?'

'Probably not, they're well concealed.'

'Who told you about them?'

'His wife. She's in the next room.'

'We'd better talk to her.'

It was a large house that reflected the status of the man. He was a vocal defender of the need for more money to be spent in the area of scientific research. Larry knew him as a blowhard, always sounding off on the television about his own importance. Wendy had seen him once or twice, always switched over to another channel. She remembered that the man had had an irritating, whining voice; it always reminded her of a foghorn, its handle slowly being cranked.

Hutton's wife sat in a chair in a room apparently reserved for guests, not used otherwise. A policewoman sat with her, the family doctor administering care. 'She's suffered a relapse, a minor heart attack,' he said.

Wendy looked at the expression on the woman's face. It was clear that she was not conscious of her surroundings. Wendy had seen the same look on her mother's face when she was dying. The doctor, a short man, pudgy around the waist, bald, had been kind in his estimation of his patient's condition. 'We'll not get anything out of Mrs Hutton,' Wendy said to Larry.

'When can we talk to Mrs Hutton?' Larry asked the doctor.

'Her condition is terminal. Her son and daughter are on their way over.'

'Shouldn't she be in a hospital?' Wendy asked.

'It's too late for that, and besides, I've known the family for years. This is where they'd choose for her to pass away, next to her husband.'

'Have you seen Mr Hutton?' Larry asked.

'Not yet.'

'Don't then. There's not much you can do in there.'

'It's what's caused the relapse. I thought she'd last another few months, but the shock...'

Larry and Wendy left the room and walked out of the front door of the house. The usual crowd was forming, smartphones at the ready, recording every event. Wendy thought them ghoulish, or maybe they didn't know what had happened in the house.

'We should be able to put a name to the murderer now,' Larry said. It was early afternoon, and the two police officers were meant to be at Challis Street for the visit of Alwyn Davies, not that either of them had any great desire to meet him. Wendy saw nothing to be gained for her: her retirement was approaching, and the rank of sergeant was as far as she was going to go. Larry still harboured hopes of making a chief inspector once Isaac moved on, and he had been attempting to study, ensure he had more qualifications to back up his promotion, although he was not too keen on meeting the commissioner. He had run across him once before at a course, where the new commissioner, as Davies was then, had given a rousing speech about modern policing, the need to maintain cordial relations with the general public, and above all to be professional. Davies's speech had been well received; all those attending had shaken his hand, had the obligatory photo taken with him. At the time, Larry had thought him to be a breath of fresh air, the sort of person to shake up the stuffy and regimented police force. However, since joining the Challis Street Homicide team he'd re-evaluated Davies, and after the DCI Caddick incident, where Caddick had temporarily occupied Isaac Cook's seat, he had decided that Commissioner Alwyn Davies was tarred with the same brush as they all were: looking out for those who sucked up to them, discarding those who just got on with their jobs.

'DCI Cook will need our support,' Wendy said. Larry knew that she had a soft spot for the man, young enough to be her son. He had to admit that his admiration for Isaac had grown by leaps and bounds ever since he had brought him into the department. At his other station, he had been dealing with a senior who wanted his people to show him the necessary deference, even when the man, a moderate performer, did not justify it. But Isaac Cook gave his team the direction they needed, was willing to listen to suggestions, as well as criticism if valid, and supported them at every opportunity.

'Let's go,' Larry said. The commissioner was due in the next thirty minutes, and he knew he'd be making a beeline for Homicide.

***

It was one of Gordon Windsor's team that found suitable quality fingerprints. For the previous two murders, there had been no proof, other than poor-quality fingerprints, of who had committed the act. But imprinted in Harold Hutton's blood, a set of fingerprints that could be used. The crime scene team took special care in making a copy and uploading it to a laptop.

'We're running a check on the fingerprints,' Windsor said on the phone to Isaac. The DCI could tell that the man was excited. Down the corridor, no more than five minutes away from

Homicide, the foreboding presence of the commissioner. Isaac had seen Davies before, never met him, and he did not like the look of him. He thought the man looked devious and menacing, although Isaac wasn't sure if that was his own prejudice. Regardless, the commissioner was about to come in the door, and his department was on its best behaviour: files correctly labelled, everyone at their desk, casually glancing at the man who could make their lives miserable, although his tenure in the job was shaky. Another terrorist attack, foiled this time, had saved him for another day, but the media, always desperate for someone to blame, had chosen Alwyn Davies.

The man who walked into Homicide, midway between Fraud and Administration, was initially pleasant. 'Detective Chief Inspector Cook, pleased to meet you,' Davies said as he shook Isaac's hand. Alongside the man stood Detective Chief Superintendent Richard Goddard, resplendent in his police officer's uniform, the gold rings around the cuffs of his jacket.

'One of our best,' Goddard said. Isaac could see the signs between the commissioner and his DCS: the frowning, the raising of an eye, the subtle hand gestures. It was clear that Goddard was trying his best, but Davies was not biting.

'There's been a few problems, DCI,' Davies said. It was evident the man did not intend to leave in a hurry.

Bridget came over. 'A cup of tea, Commissioner?' she asked.

'Don't mind if I do, milk, two sugars,' the man's reply. Isaac was annoyed; he had been trying to keep the visit short, and there was Bridget playing hostess, aiming to get through to the man with a cup of tea. Goddard continued to act as though he was interested in what Davies had to say.

'Harold Hutton?' Davies said. It was clear that the man was well informed, further confirmation that someone was slipping him updates. 'You've got a decent set of fingerprints.'

'We're attempting a match,' Isaac said.

'The man's been giving you the runaround,' Davies said. He was holding his cup of tea in one hand and had sat down at one of the desks. Down the corridor, the other recipients of his visit to Challis Street waited. Isaac had seen them out of the corner of his eye. *He's not here for you*, he thought.

'That's true,' Isaac said. Best act of defence, Isaac thought, was to defer to the man's superior wisdom.

'So what are you doing?'

'We've an all points out on the man.'

'But you don't know who he is.'

'He's changed his appearance, and why he was living as a tramp for so many years makes no sense.'

'Hutton's going to make a difference. I'm going to be asked to give answers about what we are doing to catch his murderer,' Davies said.

'It's not common knowledge yet.'

'It is where it matters. I knew the man, can't say I liked him, but he had influence, even if his politics were suspect.'

'That's as maybe, Commissioner, but we can only work on evidence. We'll place special focus on the man's death, bring in extra people if needed,' Isaac said. Goddard visibly shrank at Isaac's faux pas.

'I'd say they are needed now,' Davies said.

'I've complete confidence in DCI Cook and his team,' Goddard said.

'That's what you said when that mad woman was on the loose, and what happened there? How many did she kill? Nine or ten?'

'We stopped her in the end.' Isaac attempted to defend himself and the department.

'Only because I acted and brought in DCI Caddick. That man sharpened you up.'

Isaac could feel the tension building in him. Not only was the commissioner singing the praises of the singularly charmless DCI Caddick, but it was also clear that he, as the commissioner, had taken the credit for ending the infamous reign of Charlotte Hamilton, a serial killer without parallel in the last fifteen years.

'I'd beg to differ, Commissioner,' Isaac said. He knew that he could not sit silent and allow the man to take the credit when his team were nearby, listening in to the conversation.

'Beg as much as you like, Caddick made the difference. How many has this man killed now?'

'Three.'

'I'm not going to let this go as far as ten.'

'We're sure we'll have him soon,' Goddard said. 'I've every confidence.'

'That's what you said last time, and I let you carry on. Believe me, this time I'll act. One more murder and I'll bring in Caddick. That man knows how to get results.'

Davies stood up and walked out of the door. Isaac noticed him ignore the other departments as he strolled along the corridor. Within two minutes, he had left the building.

'He's not a bundle of fun, is he?' Larry said.

'He's still the man who controls our fate,' Isaac replied.

Goddard returned to the department. 'We've got to head this man off at the pass,' he said.

'Diplomacy's not his strong point,' Isaac said.

'The hatchets are out for him. He doesn't need to indulge in diplomacy, only to get the results. And if that means all of us, he'll not hesitate to chop us off at the knees.'

'But Caddick?'

'The commissioner's playing a strategic game. If he replaces the heads of departments, places the blame on them, he'll gain a honeymoon period; gives him another three months.'

'The end result will be worse.'

'Isaac, you'd not make it as a politician if you can't see what he's up to. The man's protecting himself, the results are dispensable.'

'He shouldn't be in his position then.'

'An admirable sentiment. Naïve, but admirable. Besides, let's not give him a chance to act. What do you have?'

Larry and Wendy, as well as Bridget, had been present when Isaac and their DCS had had their conversation, a clear sign that Goddard trusted them.

'We'll wait to see if we have a fingerprint match,' Larry said.

'And if they don't match.'

'We're compiling a dossier of Harold Hutton's associates,' Isaac said.

'The man must have had plenty,' Goddard replied.

'We realise that; that's why we'll cross-reference them against known associates of George Arbuthnot.'

'Bob Robertson?'

'That seems circumstantial. We may be wrong there, but Robertson had no government involvement and no association to Arbuthnot.'

'What's with this Arbuthnot?' Goddard asked.

'We believe that he was trading arms under the auspices of the British Government.'

'You know what that means?'

'Powerful friends. It's not the first time we've been there, is it?' Isaac said.

'Not the first time, and every time it gets mucky and dangerous. Are we opening something we might not be able to close?' Goddard asked.

Isaac could see the worry in the man's face. Yet again, he, they, were about to be thrust from a murder inquiry into involvement with the government, and each time that happened the death count went up, and not always at the hand of the primary suspect.

'Harold Hutton was into scientific research, not weapons,' Wendy said.

'Who do you think funds scientific research?' Goddard said. 'The man may have been interested in research for noble reasons, but he would have been a pragmatist; after all, he was a politician. If funding depended on directing research towards the military, he would have embraced it.'

'Reluctantly?' Isaac asked.

'Who knows? He could have been an ardent pacifist, or a man out for whatever he could for his own interests, not caring at what cost. You can research him, although you'll probably not find very much dirt on him. For whatever reason, your tramp thought that he should die, and unless Hutton's death is purely random, then he was in deep. Find the link between Hutton and Arbuthnot, and you'll find your murderer.'

Chapter 15

Ed Barrow was a worried man, and not only because he was married to Malcolm Woolston's widow. If Arbuthnot and Hutton had died, then he'd be next. The solution to the dilemma was not clear. If he told his wife, Gwen, that the man was still alive, how would she react?

Would she feel the need to transfer her emotions from him to her previous husband, Lazarus resurrected?

Malcolm Woolston had been dead for over a decade; if he continued to stay dead, at least to his wife and daughter, then all would be well, but where was the man, and would he be capable of ordering his assassination? Barrow knew the answer to the question.

It had been him that had co-signed the authorisation to detain his friend and subject him to the horrendous treatment that had been meted out to him. He had watched for some time, a morbid interest in the subjugation of one person by another. He had watched Arbuthnot and the other torturer hitting Woolston with all the force that he could muster, Arbuthnot standing close by, taking part when the first man took a break. It had only been three men in that room, the victim and the perpetrators, with a viewing hole in one wall.

Barrow could not feel any sadness at the deaths of Arbuthnot and Hutton. One was a parasite who did the bidding of others, sold weapons to governments who would use them against their own people, against other countries, other religions. And then there was Hutton, sanctimonious, expansive in his support of scientific research for the betterment of the country, the betterment of mankind, willing to make deals with the military in exchange for their funding.

It had not concerned Woolston initially, as he had believed the spiel put forward by Hutton, but he had soon sensed the ulterior motive, even spoken to Barrow about it on a few occasions. Back then, it had been Ed and Sue, Malcolm and Gwen. Sue still remained in the department, but Barrow could at least feel some pride that he had severed that relationship soon after Malcolm's death.

***

Gordon Windsor was in Isaac's office. The commissioner had left, and a relative normality had returned to Challis Street Police Station. Isaac was pleased to see the crime scene examiner, a man he regarded as a friend, although his visits to the office were rare.

'We've been able to match some of the fingerprints,' Windsor said.

'Great. There's a name?'

'No name, just a match.'

'What do you mean?'

'All details of the fingerprint's identity have been blocked on the database.'

'Who could do that?'

'It would need a court order, possible security implications.'

'Any way to break it?'

'Not a chance. The password would be encrypted. We'll never get through.'

'Your suggestion?' Isaac asked.

'The man worked for the government. There's a reference number. You've some influential contacts, people who operate behind the scenes.'

'I know some, not sure if I trust them.'

'You've no alternative. Either you get the password, or else I can't get you a name.'

'Leave it with me. I'll make a few phone calls.'

Isaac sat down and considered the situation after Windsor had left. He knew that McTavish, the former government whip, had the contacts, could even get him an answer within hours, but he no longer trusted the man. His DCS would know some other people.

Whatever way Isaac looked at it, he could see that obtaining the password had an inherent risk, possibly more damaging than the murders so far. Experience told him that once the security organisations become involved, MI5, MI6, then deaths start escalating. Some of those would become classified as well, possibly the three known murders too.

Isaac phoned his DCS, explained the situation and the need to maintain confidentiality. He assumed that Goddard would contact McTavish, but there was no alternative; they needed a confirmed name for the murderer.

Two hours later, Goddard phoned back with an update. 'The password's been removed.'

'Angus McTavish?' Isaac asked.

'I've other contacts. Someone owed me a favour.'

'He'll keep quiet?'

'I hope so.'

Isaac walked over to Bridget. He passed on the information, let her log on to Fingerprints as she was more computer savvy than him. 'Malcolm Woolston,' she said.

'Is there an address?' Isaac asked.

'According to this, he died eleven years ago. Are you certain this man is the murderer?'

'Any addresses?'

'There's one for where he worked.'

'That'll do. And update the all points. Do you have a photo?'

'It's old, but I'll use it,' Bridget said.

***

Ed Barrow did not appreciate the presence of two police officers in his office. He had just made a phone call to resolve the problem, and now he was being questioned about the same subject. The situation was precarious, he knew that. One wrong word, one incorrect response, and the police would smell a rat.

His best response, he thought, was to be as honest as he could while bypassing the details, claiming privileged knowledge, although he wasn't sure if any of it would work.

And then, what about his wife? What if she found out that her long-dead husband was back and he was killing people? Would she believe him, or would she believe the police? He had seen her looking at her first husband's photo on more than one occasion; there was even a framed picture in their bedroom of father and daughter. The child had only been six months old then, and now she was married with a child of a similar age. What if the officers questioned her? What would she say? What could she say?

'I'm Detective Chief Inspector Isaac Cook,' Isaac said. He was glad to be out of the office. Wendy was chasing up on Malcolm Woolston's whereabouts, working with Bridget to access bank accounts, driving licence records, anything that could give them a clue as to where the man was. Larry was with Isaac; both had shown their IDs.

'What can I do for you?' Barrow asked.

Isaac looked at the man before responding, aiming to get his measure: his body language, perspiration on the forehead, any tell-tale signs that the man was about to lie.

'Malcolm Woolston,' Isaac said, watching for the response.

Too measured, too calculating, too calm, Isaac thought as he observed the man.

'It's a long time since I've heard that name mentioned. The man's dead; tragic accident.'

'Accident? I thought it was suicide,' Isaac said.

'You're right, a suicide. They only ever found his clothes and a clear indication that he had swum out from the beach.'

'But no body?'

'Why the interest? It's been ten, eleven years.'

'You should know; you married his widow.'

'There's a few years separation between the two events. Malcolm had been declared legally dead before we married.'

'With no body?'

'It's all in the judge's summation. The water temperature was close to freezing, the man would have succumbed to the cold within a short period of time, and there was an outgoing tide. The evidence was not disputed.'

'And his wife?'

'She was upset for a few years, but time moves on.'

'And then you married her?'

'You make it sound indecent. Malcolm and I were good friends, as was Gwen, my wife. It only seemed natural that I should be there for her; I even walked their daughter down the aisle some years later.'

'Tell us about Malcolm Woolston,' Larry said. He'd taken the opportunity to look around the office. It all seemed functional: a desk, Barrow's chair with its back to the window, a bookcase in one corner, a computer terminal and a printer on another desk. The man apparently appreciated the finer things in life. On the wall was what appeared to be an original oil painting.

'What do you do here?' Isaac asked.

'We're a small government-funded research department.'

'What type of research?'

'Some of it's classified, but what's this got to do with Malcolm?'

'He's still alive,' Isaac said.

'Impossible,' Barrow said, standing up from his chair.

'We have proof.'

'How?'

'He murdered George Arbuthnot and Harold Hutton. You do know both of these men?'

'Well, yes. But why? And how do you know he's alive? We've all believed him to be dead for years.'

'Fingerprints.'

'They can be faked, can't they?'

'You're the scientist, you tell us,' Isaac said.

'I suppose so, but why?'

'The evidence pointing to this department is indisputable. Whatever the reason for Arbuthnot and Hutton, whatever the reason for Woolston returning, the answers lie here.'

'I don't know what you're talking about. This is all too much for me to take in.'

'We came here first. Woolston's wife and daughter need to be told.'

'Please, not yet. You can imagine the effect this will have on them. It may be best if I tell them.'

'That is your prerogative, but we will need to talk to your wife soon.'

'Give me two days.'

'Coming back to Malcolm Woolston,' Isaac said. 'Why did he disappear?'

'What do you know about the man?' Barrow asked.

'At this present moment, not a lot. We're compiling a dossier. We know he was brilliant, with many academic papers to his name, and engineering and mathematics doctorates.'

'The man was impressive. He was the smartest man I knew, and I've met a few over the years.'

'Anything more?'

'You'll find this out soon enough.'

'What?'

'Malcolm Woolston was brilliant, and as with all brilliant men, he was subject to eccentricity.'

'What sort of eccentricity?'

'He was a genius level intellect bordering on madness. He'd been hospitalised a few times in the past. You'll find that out if you check. He had a persecution complex, and he could be violent.'

'Any instances here?'

'He tried it on me once; suspected me of strangling his research budget.'

'Were you?'

'The department was being subjected to another financial audit. I had to clamp down on expenditure to make the books balance. It wasn't aimed at Malcolm, although he saw it that way.'

'What was he researching?'

'Classified. Way above your level.'

'I could get clearance,' Isaac said.

'You must understand, I'm subject to the Official Secrets Act. It would be a criminal offence for me to reveal what he was working on.'

Isaac did not believe the man, but he had been forced to sign the Official Secrets Act, as had Larry, when they had been looking for a missing woman in a previous case.

However, Malcolm Woolston did not appear to be involved with the security organisations, but was purely a man out for revenge, and if he had killed Arbuthnot and Hutton for that reason, then Barrow was a clear target as well.

The first thing that Isaac intended to resolve was to get the necessary security clearance. He was sure he would be back in Barrow's office after that, and as for his wife, he would not wait for Barrow to inform her that she had two husbands, both alive and well.

Isaac knew he'd take Wendy on that occasion.

Outside in the street, Larry asked, 'What do you reckon?'

'Scientific research, an arms dealer. What do you think?'

'I'd say they were researching advanced weaponry. That would explain the security rating.'

'Maybe,' Isaac said. 'These people all tend to be neurotic.'

'Ed Barrow?'

'Until he's been checked out, he remains suspect. Whatever happens, he's a prime target.'

Inside the building, Barrow picked up his phone. Sue Christie was sitting alongside him. 'The police have identified Malcolm Woolston.'

'We'll implement damage control. You were right to doubt his disappearance all those years ago, but, where was he?'

'The question is not where he was; the question is where he is now,' Barrow said.

114

He hung up the phone and turned to Sue Christie. 'This is going to get dirty. Are you prepared for the flak?'

'I'm prepared,' she said as she leant over and kissed him firmly on the lips.

Chapter 16

Malcolm Woolston, no longer using the name of Big Greg, realised that he was navigating a tricky path. On one side, the need to protect the results of his research and to extract his revenge. On the other, the need to be with his family again. He knew why he had killed Robertson; he had had enough of living a lie, hiding in the shadows, pretending to be someone he was not.

A methodical man, he laid out the plan on his laptop. He had dealt with those who had tortured him, and he had lined up his wife's second husband as another person who had to die. He assumed that the man, callous as he knew him to be, would not have told Gwen, that her first husband, Malcolm, was alive and well, and close by.

He had given the police a warning, not that he had ever expected them to take heed. He had seen the black police inspector with the woman from the hostel that he had spoken to on the bench. Very friendly he had thought when he had seen them, but then, he knew her history, had seen her selling herself.

It was strange, he thought, that when he had been disreputable and on the street the thought of the soft touch of a woman had not entered his mind, although it did now, but it was always the same woman: his wife. And she was safely ensconced with Ed Barrow, one of the men he had decided to kill. Maybe if he explained all that had happened, all that must occur, then she would transfer her affections back to him.

He knew that was unlikely. Too much water under the bridge, too much anguish and sorrow, too many deaths, and after he had disposed of Ed, there would only be revulsion, bitterness, recriminations. They had been happy years with his wife and their daughter, but they were in the past, and now there was only the future. A future that looked bleak and empty.

***

Ed Barrow knew that the situation was tenuous. For almost
fifteen years he had held the position of director of the research
department. With that had come an appreciable salary complete
with benefits: the car, the superannuation, the budget to continue
with the projects that interested him. Regardless of how Malcolm
Woolston saw him, he knew that he was a decent man who had
been placed in a difficult position. There had only been one
option that fateful day when the two men had visited him: he
agreed to the military men's demands, or they'd ensure the
department was closed down and he would be evicted from the
building.

It was as if it was only yesterday, when he and Sue,
Malcolm, and Gwen would spend most summer Sunday
afternoons barbequing or taking trips to the sea for the day. He
had envied his friend with his perfect wife and his perfect child.

He knew he could never have what Malcolm had, it was
not possible medically, and Sue, an attractive woman in her
thirties then, a lot of fun, physically very demanding, was not
interested either. They had discussed marriage, but she was not
overly keen. 'I like to keep my options open,' she had said.

Ed knew that what she meant was that she liked the
freedom to date other men, to sleep with them, to discard them.
Sue was an independent woman, he knew that, and he had always
realised that she was not wife material, but he had asked her
anyway. They had been together two years by that time, and the
openness had been more on her side than his.

He knew that he had been disturbed that day when they
had grabbed Malcolm as he was preparing to leave the building,
after he had made it clear to everyone that he had solved the final
problem and that he was able to create energy at minimal cost,
limitless energy in his estimation.

He had watched Arbuthnot and the other man laying into
his friend the following day until he had become too sickened to
watch. He had seen Harold Hutton countersign the documents

with him on behalf of his government for the treatment to continue, and now Hutton and Arbuthnot were both dead. And now Malcolm was coming for him and, no doubt, for Sue.

He loved Gwen, he knew that, and with Malcolm's death, the field had been clear for him to press his suit with her. He remembered how Gwen had reacted that first time, six months after Malcolm had disappeared. That had not been a good day when he confronted her in the kitchen of her house, told her how he felt. She had reacted with a gentle rebuke, then with soulful sobbing for the husband who was not coming back. He had tried to put his arms around her to comfort her, but she pushed him away.

He had left that house that day with her in tears, telling him not to come back. It was another three months before he saw her again, and the tears had stopped. As she said, she had to remain strong for their daughter. For nearly two years, they kept in touch, his helping as he could, sometimes acting as a substitute for the child's father, sometimes babysitting while Gwen ventured out into the world of dating again.

One night when she had come home late, complaining that her date had drunk too much, made too many offensive remarks, they had ended up naked on the floor. The young child, by that time thirteen going on fourteen, was fast asleep upstairs. It was only the second time that he had told Gwen that he loved her, and he wanted to be with her and Malcolm's daughter. They married two months later, a quiet ceremony in a local registry office, a reception back at the house, a honeymoon in the Canary Islands, the daughter accompanying them.

And now Malcolm was back, and to complicate matters, he knew about Sue. If he knew how to access Ed's laptop and to switch on the camera, he must have seen them making love in the office.

Ed knew he had tried, and for three years he had resisted the advances of his former lover, but she could not be dissuaded. 'I need to be loved,' she had said.

Eventually, he had given in and slept with her once again. In the years that followed, their coupling would be an accepted

118

routine every Thursday night when the office was quiet, and everyone else had gone home. Once back home, later than usual, his dinner would be on the table, Gwen smiling, happy to see him, never suspecting, never questioning.

***

The cameras at Harold Hutton's house had been effective. For the first time, the Homicide department had a clear picture of the man who had knocked on the door. Not only that, the man had not been wearing a cap.

'Malcolm Woolston,' Bridget said. 'I've compared the old and the new photos, they match.'

'Good work,' Isaac replied, temporarily distracted by DCS Goddard on the phone.

'Are you certain?' Wendy asked.

'Ninety-five per cent,' Bridget's reply.

'Did you get that, sir?' Isaac said into the mic on his phone.

'Keep me posted. I'll make sure the commissioner knows.'

'Best of luck.'

'With that man!'

***

Sue Christie was the first to see them as they entered the building. She was soon in Ed Barrow's office. 'It's the police,' she said.

'Again. They were here yesterday,' Barrow's reply. 'How do we handle this?'

'Act natural.'

Sue left Barrow's office, giving him a few minutes to prepare himself. She walked out to the landing on the second floor of the building. 'Can I help you?' she said.

'I'm DCI Cook, this is my colleague, DI Hill. We've a few more questions for Mr Barrow.'

'He'll be free in a few minutes. Can I help you in the interim? I'm Mr Barrow's personal assistant.'

'You weren't here on our first visit. We're interested in an employee that used to work here,' Isaac said.

The three moved to a room outside Barrow's office.

'Maybe I can help,' Sue Christie said. Isaac had to admit she was a fine-looking woman, a little older than him but dressed well, capable, judging by her orderly desk and the files at the back of it neatly labelled A to Z.

'This man left here eleven years ago, suddenly.'

'I've been here for fifteen, almost the same length as Mr Barrow.'

'Malcolm Woolston, do you remember him?'

'It's a long time, but yes. I was friends with him and his wife. Why do you ask? He died a long time ago.'

'He died under mysterious circumstances.'

'Yes, I know. We were all so shocked when he died. They never found his body, but I assume you know that. Why is it so important?'

'Malcolm Woolston is not dead,' Larry said.

'Mr Barrow told me what you had said to him yesterday, but it's not possible; we all attended his funeral.'

'But with no body?'

'They called it a remembrance service in his memory.'

'We have proof that he is still alive,' Isaac said. 'We need to contact him immediately.'

Sue Christie laughed, a nervous laugh, Larry observed.

'Has he contacted this office?' Isaac asked.

'He's dead, we all know he is.'

'We?'

'Everyone, Mr Barrow, his wife, the staff here.'

'His wife?'

'Three years after Malcolm disappeared, he married his widow.'

'Mr Barrow told us that last time. It must be complicated.'

'Why? We were all friends. Malcolm was gone, and Gwen, that's his wife, was lonely. The two made a great match. He brought up Malcolm's daughter as if she was his own.'

'Is Mr Barrow free?'

The woman left and went into the adjoining office. She closed the door behind her. Two minutes later, Ed Barrow reopened the door and invited the two police officers in.

'Harold Hutton?' Larry asked.

'We spoke about this yesterday,' Ed Barrow said. 'Are you certain Malcolm was involved in his death?'

'We are,' Isaac said.

'Harold Hutton was here last month. And even if Malcolm is still alive, why would he want to kill Hutton? The man has done a lot for the country, no skeletons in his cupboard.'

'The man's death was violent. We can place Malcolm Woolston at the crime scene.'

'Malcolm was a pacifist. He'd not harm a fly.'

'A fly, maybe not, but three men now.'

'It can't be Malcolm. It must be someone who looks like him.'

'We can confirm that Malcolm Woolston is a mass murderer. He's killed one person with a direct connection to this department, and another who you've admitted to knowing.'

'George Arbuthnot?'

'Yes.'

'I told you last time that I'd met him, but only at a function somewhere. He's not been here.'

'Mr Barrow,' Isaac said, 'we will make a connection between George Arbuthnot and Harold Hutton. If a connection exists to this department as well, we will find out, rest assured. Hutton was interested in scientific research. Arbuthnot, from what we can tell, dealt in military weapons.'

'Our research is for the benefit of mankind, not its destruction,' Barrow said.

'Although some of your projects could be converted to military purposes?'

'I suppose so, but I'd resist if they ever tried it.'

'We need to know if Malcolm Woolston contacts your wife.'

'After so many years? Why now?'

'The answer to that question lies with the reason that he is on a murdering spree. Mr Barrow, are you on his list?'

Ed Barrow shifted in his seat. 'With Malcolm, you never knew what he was thinking.'

Chapter 17

Bridget busied herself in the office compiling a dossier on Malcolm Woolston, including last known address, family and where they were, friends, and whether he had been drawing a pension or an allowance from somewhere.

Isaac and Larry were back in the office, unsure about their encounter with Ed Barrow and Sue Christie. 'What do you reckon?' Larry asked.

'Not much to say. They answered the questions correctly, and there's no proof that they're on Woolston's hit list.'

'Anything more on Arbuthnot?'

'Apart from what we know, not a lot. I'm certain he's tied in somewhere with the research department, but there's no way of proving it, and if he were involved in shady arms dealing, government sponsored or not, we'd not get any help from Barrow.'

'How about his personal assistant?'

'Something is going on there,' Isaac said.

'You sensed it as well?'

'Just a little too cosy, that's all. It may be platonic, but…'

'And he's married to Woolston's widow. The man disappeared for a reason, not necessarily because he wanted to desert his family. If he suspects Barrow of playing around, cheating on his wife, then his reaction could be unpredictable.'

'Nothing unpredictable about how he killed Hutton and Arbuthnot.'

'Commissioner Davies wants Hutton's killer apprehended soon.'

'Has DCS Goddard been on the phone again?' Larry asked.

'It's understandable. Hutton was well known, well respected. There were even condolences in the House of Commons by the prime minister.'

'We still don't know why he's come back. After so many years, you'd think he would have stayed hidden.'

'Something caused him to resurface.'

'He'll kill again.'

'But who? Barrow, Sue Christie, even his wife for marrying someone else?'

'We'll need to make contact with her, tell her to be on the lookout.'

'We told Barrow we'd give him two days.'

'It can't wait. The woman needs protection.'

***

It was two in the afternoon; Ed Barrow had been forewarned. Isaac Cook and Wendy Gladstone presented themselves at the Barrow residence. Ed Barrow opened the door. 'I've told my wife that you are coming.'

'Did you tell her why?'

'No. I've also asked her daughter to be present.'

'She's here?'

'Yes.'

The two police officers entered the house, recently renovated from what Isaac could see. In the main room, two women sat. 'I'm Gwen Barrow, this is my daughter, Sally.'

In the other room, a child could be heard. 'She should be alright for a few minutes,' the younger of the two women said. Wendy could see that she was a bright woman, early-twenties, with dark hair. On her left hand she wore a wedding ring.

The similarities between the two women were striking.

'Mrs Barrow,' Isaac said. He realised that it was going to be difficult.

'Call me Gwen. Mrs Barrow makes me sound old.'

'Gwen, has your husband told you the reason we are here?'

'Only that it has something to do with Malcolm.'

'That is correct. What I am to tell you will be distressing.'

'It was a long time ago. I've no more tears, neither has Sally.'

Isaac realised he was procrastinating. He took a deep breath. 'Malcolm Woolston did not die eleven years ago.'

'What do you mean? Ed, did you know about this?'

'They told me earlier.'

'When, if it wasn't when we thought it was?' Sally asked. The child was making a noise in the other room. 'Susie needs her bottle,' she said.

'I'll deal with it. You need to be here,' Wendy said.

After Wendy had left and the child had quietened down, Isaac continued. 'Malcolm Woolston is not dead.'

The two women sat up straight; the older of the two, the colour in her face draining away.

'How, why?' Sally asked.

'Malcolm Woolston, we now know, has been near to this house and in the area for the last five to six years, probably longer.'

'We would have seen him,' Gwen Barrow said.

'You would not have recognised him.'

'Why not? I was married to the man for thirteen years.'

'Believe me,' Isaac said, 'this must be very difficult, but we have proof that he has been in the area, and that he is very much alive as we speak.'

'Then why does he hide?'

'Let me ask you both. Have either of you ever seen a homeless man in the area?'

'I have on many occasions,' Sally said. 'I even gave him some money, some food, but why?'

'Describe him?'

'Dirty, unkempt. He smelt bad.'

'Was he tall or short?'

'He was sitting down the one time I approached him, but he was probably tall.'

'Anything else?'

'Not really. I noticed him looking at us a few times. He wanted to say hello to Susie once.'

'Did you let him?'

'No. I didn't want him spreading germs over her. She had a bit of a cough as it was.'

'Have you,' Isaac asked, 'seen another man, casually dressed in a pair of trousers, a jacket, with short hair and a black beard?'

'He wanted to give a sweet to Susie. I threatened to call the police.'

'What do you reckon?' Isaac asked Wendy who had just returned to the room.

'Gwen, Sally, we are sure that those two men were one and the same; they were Malcolm Woolston,' Wendy said.

'We have a photo,' Isaac said. He handed the picture to the two women. They both looked at it for several minutes. Gwen Barrow seemed close to passing out. Ed Barrow had his arm around her.

Sally held the photo firm, her hand shaking. 'That's him,' she said. 'That's the man in the park.'

'He's also your father.'

'But why?' Gwen Barrow asked.

'We don't know why he disappeared, but we are aware that he has returned.'

'Is this a police matter?' Sally asked.

'Unfortunately, it is. We're from Homicide. There's a warrant out for his arrest,' Isaac said.

'Is he suspected of murder?' Gwen Barrow asked.

'He must be regarded as dangerous, and at no time must you allow yourselves to come into direct contact with him.'

'Will he harm us?'

'We don't think so, but we do not understand his motives as to why he stayed hidden for all this time, and we've not figured out why he has committed murder.'

'How many?' Ed Barrow asked, although he had already been told the answer.

'Three that we know of.'

'He can't have done what you say,' Sally said. 'Not my father.'

'We have proof. He will be arrested. You must understand that,' Isaac said.

'We both understand, DCI. Thank you for coming to tell us personally,' Gwen Barrow said. She was holding her daughter tight.

***

Isaac had always thought that the most difficult part of policing was telling the relatives that a loved one had died in an unfortunate accident, but he had been wrong. Sitting in that house telling Malcolm Woolston's former wife and his daughter that the man was a mass murderer was much worse. And now they still had to find the man, charge him, convict him, and then lock him up.

Once he had had to tell a decent, law-abiding couple that their youngest son had blown himself up, along with some innocent bystanders. As tragic as that had been, the perpetrator, as well as his victims, were dead, and in time mourned and then compartmentalised in the minds of their relatives. Those people had been allowed to continue with their lives, fractured as they may have been, but with Malcolm Woolston, the man would be around forever, and there'd be the soul-searching by his wife about what she may have done wrong to cause him to disappear. And then the conflicting loyalties and loves of two men, both husbands. And as for the daughter, the father she had cherished with a childhood memory was no longer a man to be proud of, but a man who killed others.

Isaac knew the future for Gwen Barrow and her daughter would be troubled.

Back in the office, Isaac had no time to dwell on such matters. Malcolm Woolston had been identified by his daughter who had seen him several times as a homeless man, once in his

127

more recent guise. Both the women needed protection. Isaac organised two uniforms to be placed close to their respective houses, and for police cars to patrol their neighbourhoods. Not that they were total protection, and if the man could change from homeless to casual respectable, he could transform yet again. His motives were still unclear, although the research department seemed to be the key location.

Isaac and Larry drove out there again. It was not the most attractive building in London, Isaac would admit that, but inside it was state of the art. Sue Christie met them on arrival, accorded them a warm welcome, showed them around. They saw where Woolston had worked years before, but as she said, back then it wasn't as good as they saw it now.

'What about the staff?' Isaac asked. 'Any from that period?'

'There's one or two, but Helen Toogood is probably the person to talk to.'

Ed Barrow was not in the building, which suited Isaac fine. And besides, he didn't trust him. It was clear that Gwen Barrow relied on him heavily, and that his stepdaughter had shown a fondness for him, but the man wasn't clean yet.

Isaac and Larry were sitting in one of the laboratories when Helen Toogood entered. The two men stood and shook her hand. She was a small woman, not up to Isaac's shoulder, with a timid voice. She sat down; her hands were folded across her front, almost in a defensive mode.

'Mrs Toogood, you were here when Malcolm Woolston disappeared, is that correct?'

'Very sad, very sad,' she said.

'What can you tell us about him?'

'Without him our research floundered.'

'What were you researching?'

'Low-cost energy. The ability to generate vast quantities of energy for minimal cost.'

'Has that research finished?'

'We still work on it, but we've not solved some fundamental problems.'

128

'What problems? And please, we're not technical people.'

'The energy we could produce was unstable, as well as difficulties with the directional controls of the beam from the solar collectors in low-level orbit. Instead of solar panels on earth, we'd place them in space. It's extremely complicated, and it requires men of Malcolm's genius to solve the outstanding problems. More likely to blow up than drive a turbine.'

'This beam, is it dangerous?' Isaac asked.

'Not really, it's microwave. Laser rays from space are for science fiction. If a bird flew over the ground-based receiver, it may have been fried.'

'Could it have become a weapon?'

'The energy could be channelled for that purpose. That wasn't our area of research, though.'

'And you needed Malcolm Woolston to provide the solution to the outstanding issues?'

'It's always been too expensive, and then the directional control has been complex, but Malcolm had solved both issues.'

'Complicated?'

'It needed a genius-level intellect. The formulation, the technical expertise required was beyond me.'

'Did it take a lot of space?'

'For generating large-scale electricity, although a condensed version could have been put on a missile. As I said, the solution was with Malcolm. He could have completed it, but we've not been able to emulate his results, and we have access to much more powerful computers.'

'Does a lot of your research produce results as dramatic?'

'Not really, but if you can produce energy, you can produce destruction. Basic physics. It was straightforward for Malcolm; for us, it became too complicated, and then he disappeared. One day he's here, the next he's gone. And then, a few weeks afterwards, he's dead.'

'What was the reaction here when he died?'

'We were shocked, I can tell you that.'

Isaac could see that the woman spent too much time in a laboratory. Her skin was pallid, her hair tied back in an unfashionably severe style. On her feet, she wore sensible shoes, which made sense, as he had noticed that the tiled floor was slippery, apart from the rubber mats placed at strategic points. He did not like the place; it reminded him of the science department at his old school.

'How did it affect the project he was working on?'

'They expected us to carry on without him, but it was not possible. Malcolm was the genius, not us. In the end, we put it to one side.'

'The project was shelved?'

'We've never been able to solve what Malcolm was working on. And now, it's not so relevant.'

'What do you mean?'

'Back then, it was coal and oil-fired power stations, fuel-guzzling cars.'

'And now?'

'Earth-based solutions have improved, although the energy from space remains viable. And besides, the budget's not there anymore. Everything's incredibly expensive, and without money there's not much we can do, except theorise.'

'Would the money have been available for Malcolm Woolston?'

'Oh, yes. I used to see them with Ed Barrow.'

'Who?'

'The men with the money.'

'Do you know who they were?'

'I know one of them was an army man.'

'Others?'

'Just before Malcolm disappeared there were a few.'

'Military?'

'That's what I think.'

'Would you remember who they were?'

'I was never introduced.'

'I've a photo. Could you please look at it and tell me if you know this man?'

130

Isaac withdrew from his pocket two of the photos that Larry had found at Arbuthnot's. He showed them to Helen Toogood. She studied the first, a quick reply. 'That's Harold Hutton,' she said.

'We're aware that he was here on a regular basis.'

'He's dead. I read about it. Supposedly he was murdered.'

'He was,' Larry said.

'And the other?' Isaac asked.

The woman took out a magnifying glass from the pocket of her lab coat. She moved it up and down as she scanned the photo.'

'I never met him, but he was here once.'

'It was a long time ago; are you sure?' Larry asked.

'Quite certain. I never forget a face.'

Isaac and Larry realised that they had the second connection to the research department and to Ed Barrow and Sue Christie.

'Thank you, Mrs Toogood,' Isaac said. 'If we've any more questions, we'll be in touch.' The woman left the lab where Isaac and Larry were sitting.

Larry spoke first. 'She's identified George Arbuthnot,' he said.

'It's not conclusive, but we should be able to confront Barrow with it, see what his reaction is.'

'He'll stonewall.'

'Sue Christie's here. We'll ask her.'

The two men walked backed down the corridor to the personal assistant's office. They knocked and entered. 'Any help?' the woman asked from behind her desk.

'Are you able to help us identify a man if we show you a photo?'

'I'll try.'

Isaac handed over the photo. Sue Christie took her time in answering. 'Sorry, I don't remember him.'

'And when is Mr Barrow back?'

'No idea.'

The two police officers left soon after and found a café. 'What do you reckon?' Isaac asked.

'I'd trust Helen Toogood more than Sue Christie,' Larry said.

'That's as maybe, but Mrs Toogood's eyesight is not so sharp. You saw how she used the magnifying glass.'

'I'd still trust her first. She's got no axe to grind, whereas Barrow and his personal assistant have.'

'What do you mean?'

'Maybe not an axe. Barrow's involved with his PA. They'll cover for each other.'

'And Gwen Barrow?'

'Ed Barrow could be genuine in his affection for her, although it doesn't stop him having a bit on the side.'

'Are we confident that he is?' Isaac asked.

'It's not relevant, not yet, if he is.'

'True, but it raises the question of why Ed Barrow married the widow: out of love or to keep a watch out for Woolston.'

'It's conjecture, but I'd say the latter.'

Chapter 18

Malcolm Woolston had seen the two police officers at his former wife's house. He realised the significance: they had identified him. He had hoped it would take longer, but it did not matter. He knew that Ed Barrow hadn't called the police to let them know that a murderer was on the loose, and it wouldn't have been Sue Christie, bitch that she was. He knew all about her and her men. She had tried it on with him once, but he hadn't been interested. There was only one woman for him, Gwen, and now she was with another man and that man was cheating on her.

Woolston walked the short distance to his daughter's house, saw her arriving there two hours after the police officers had left her mother's house. Ed Barrow had driven her. He wanted to go over and confront the man, announce his return to his daughter, but it was clear that she already knew. He planned how to meet her, knowing full well her reaction.

He realised that if they knew he was back, they probably were aware of his appearance. He returned to his flat, shaved off his beard, as well as his remaining hair, and left. It was not the ideal disguise, he knew, but it would suffice. He returned to his daughter's house. A uniformed policeman was standing outside. He waited for his daughter to leave, knowing that in the park he would not be recognised.

After two hours Sally emerged. She said hello to the uniformed policeman and crossed the road, her daughter in a pushchair. She looked as if she had been crying.

'Hello,' Woolston said, as Sally sat down next to him on the only bench available.

'Hello.' A curt reply.

'I'll never harm you or your mother, believe me.'

Sally sat rigidly on the spot, unsure what to say. The young child in the pushchair played with a small toy.

'I need you to let me explain,' Woolston said.

'But, but…'

'Don't speak, just let me talk. Let me tell you how much I love you and your mother. How much I regret the years apart, the years of deception, and why it has been necessary.'

'I can't,' Sally spluttered, uncertain whether to scream or to be overjoyed. 'You've killed people.'

'I've also saved countless thousands, but they'll never tell you that. They don't care about the truth, only the lies they perpetrate.'

'Why did you vanish? You can't realise how hard it was on mum. For years she was sad. She's married again.'

'I know. I saw her and Ed at the registry office. I saw you at school, getting drunk, making a fool of yourself. I even helped you home once, but you don't remember. I was always there for you and your mother.'

'I'm not sure what to say,' Sally said. The child dropped the toy. Woolston leaned down and picked it up.

'Can I?'

'Yes. This is Susie.'

'I know.' Woolston gave the child the toy; she took it, momentarily touching his hand.

'She looks like you,' Sally said.

'I'm sorry for all the pain. I did what was necessary.'

'But all those years, and now they want you for murder.'

'The people that died, some were evil, some were good, but the secret had to be kept.'

'Why?'

'I perfected a way of generating vast amounts of low-cost energy.'

'Mum said you were involved with research.'

'My research was for peaceful purposes, but others wanted to use it for evil. I could not let them.'

'Is that why you disappeared?'

'Yes. I had to. They maltreated me.'

'Who?'

'The two men that died.'

'Is Ed involved?'

'Yes.'

'Please don't harm him. He's been good to mum and me.'

'I will leave him alone for now.'

'Would you kill him?'

'I will not let my knowledge fall into their hands. They would use it one day for the wrong reason. The consequences are too frightening.'

Across the road, the policeman at the door observed the woman that he was protecting talking to a man. He decided to investigate, although his order had been to stand at the woman's front door during the day, a particularly tedious task. The constable crossed the road and made towards Sally and her father.

Malcolm Woolston stood up and walked away. Sally moved towards the policeman. 'Is it all right?' he asked.

'Fine, thank you.'

As she went back into her house, she looked over at the park; her father was gone. She considered contacting her mother, but for some reason she did not. She had felt safe with the man, even his granddaughter had smiled at him. She knew he would not harm them.

***

Ed Barrow returned to his office the day after the revelation that his wife's former husband was still alive. He was confident that no one suspected that he already knew, even before the police officers had visited him in his office.

Sue Christie was soon in his office. She flung her arms around his neck to give him an early morning kiss. He pulled back. 'Why?' she asked.

'Sorry, there's too much going on. Don't you see it? We're targeted as well.'

'Why me?'

'Why not? You were here when he contacted me, and he knows about our affair.'

'It's your affair, not mine. You went and married Gwen, not me.'

'You know I had to.'

'Doing your duty for Queen and country?'

'We had to know if he ever contacted her.'

'You signed the initial order authorising Malcolm's torture. The man was brutal with him. I'm with Malcolm on that one. But why us? Why me?'

'Malcolm's mind could be disturbed. If he's settling old debts, then we could be drawn in. He knows that we're here making love. He's probably got videos. What if he shows Gwen?'

'He'll not do that. He was always devoted to her, you know that. Remember that time when we'd had a few too many drinks, and I sat on his lap,' Sue said.

'You were looking for a foursome.'

'I was just joking.'

'But if they had agreed?'

'I'd have been game, so would you, don't deny it.'

'It didn't happen, and Malcolm was sure angry for you suggesting it.'

'He'll not harm her; he'll not harm you, because of her.'

'You weren't here,' Ed said,' when they went to work on Malcolm.'

'You told me afterwards.'

'I told you too much.'

***

Malcolm Woolston had made a promise, a promise he could not keep indefinitely. His daughter was right in that she wanted to protect her mother from further anguish, but then his daughter was idealistic, saw the world through rose-coloured glasses.

Ed Barrow was a malignant parasite who had sold out to the highest bidder. The man sat in a decent office, with a personal assistant and a hefty salary; blood money as Woolston saw it.

He looked out of the window of his flat. A couple of children played down below, a dog barked in the distance, yet in his small flat there was nothing. The television no longer interested him, the food that he had bought had gone stale. In the past, when he had been with Gwen and Sally, he had enjoyed preparing the evening meal whenever Gwen came in late, even picking their daughter up from school. But now, he had nothing, not a noise, not a friendly face.

He looked around the flat. It was dull and devoid of reading material. Not that he wanted to read; too many ideas swirling in his mind, too many unfinished equations, too many people still alive who should not be.

Unable to sit down, Woolston left the flat and returned to where the chance of his being recognised was at its greatest. He walked past his daughter's house, past his wife's house. He could see her through the kitchen window. He thought she still looked lovely. He continued walking for several hours, finally arriving at Sue Christie's address. The woman was not there, he could tell that. He walked around the back of the building, peered in the window, saw the cat that she had had eleven years before, although it was now looking old.

**

Ed Barrow knew that Sue had been correct. Initially, he had been close to Gwen out of a feeling of compassion for her, coupled with the more immediate reason for finding out where her husband had gone. It was clear after six months that she had no idea where he was, only a belief that he was dead. With Malcolm's disappearance, he realised that he loved the woman. Sue was fun, and always ready to be laid, but with Gwen it was romance, a bottle of wine, and candles.

Sue was Thursday night in the office, or in the back seat of his car, or wherever. He liked her, and although she could be irritating, he still could not resist.

Ed knew that Malcolm was a liability, not only for the department but for his life. Eleven years earlier, it had been him who had postulated that Woolston's disappearance had been an elaborately constructed hoax.

The research still remained uncompleted; others had tried, only one person looked as though she may succeed. Ed realised that Liz Hardcastle had not fallen off the platform at the railway station; she had been pushed.

***

'What is the response from Barrow? Have you been keeping a watch on him?' a man in uniform said.

'We should have told him that Malcolm Woolston was back when we saw his formula on the internet.'

'Hindsight, pure hindsight,' the man said as he drank his brandy.

It was not often that the two men met. One was a minister of the Crown, the other, a general. In a gentlemen's club in Mayfair, their conversation would be confidential. It was a club that had figured in history, where great men had met to discuss business and war and politics, but this time the two men, separated in age by no more than two years, discussed Malcolm Woolston, the most significant research scientist and mathematician in the country, at least to them.

'Woolston could have had a knighthood by now,' General Claude Smythe said. The second son of a duke, he had chosen the army over politics. His brother, Cameron, the first son, the secretary of state for defence, sat opposite.

'That's the trouble with these idealistic fools,' Claude Smythe said. 'They somehow believe that the best security for this country, the world, is if we all universally disarm and live together in peace and harmony.'

'When the strength is in having the ultimate deterrent,' his brother replied. Since the formulas had been discovered on the internet, their meetings had become more regular. Neither man was idealistic, not even men of the people. As the sons of a duke they believed in their superior breeding. Men such as Woolston were expendable unless they had something to offer, something that would benefit them.

'Do we take Barrow into our confidence?' Claude Smythe asked.

'The man went and married Woolston's widow. Can he be trusted?'

'Uncertain.'

'Expendable?'

'If he makes the wrong decisions.'

'Is that likely?'

'We've kept a watch on him over the years. He'd been instructed to keep a watch on the man's wife, see if he had kept a record of his work somewhere, but what does he do?'

'He beds the damn woman and then marries her. Even offered to adopt her daughter.'

'The wife and daughter, can we use them as levers?'

'Why not. What do a couple of women matter?'

'The weapon is more important. We need Woolston alive.'

'The police want him arrested.'

'Pressure can be brought to bear.'

'You'd do that?'

'Why not? The defence of the realm is at stake here. Do we care that Woolston has committed murder?'

'Getting rid of Hutton was a benefit to us. Woolston saved us the trouble.'

Chapter 19

Gwen Barrow was disturbed by all that had happened. She knew that she had married Ed out of loneliness, and although she loved him, it was not the same as the passion that she had felt for Malcolm. Back then, they had been young and carefree, optimistic for the future, discussing a family, and then Sally had come along. Both of them had loved her equally, but then there had been the rough years when their daughter had strayed off the track and had found bad men and bad drugs, a result of Malcolm not being there for her.

She knew she should feel anger for what he had put them all through, but she was confused by the love that she still felt. Now he was around again, had been around for years. She wondered if he had seen her making a fool of herself the first few times she had tried the dating market. She hoped he hadn't. She felt embarrassed about what he might have seen, her attempts at relieving the sexual frustrations that she felt, the inappropriate men, the inappropriate places. If he could remain hidden for so long, then he had probably seen her, presumably seen their daughter making the same mistakes.

Where had he been? Was he watching her now? She looked out of the window. A couple on the other side of the road, a child on the way home from school, a man of about the right age but not tall enough. She knew she was concerning herself with a man who had died in her mind, not in her heart, a decade previously, and now he was back, and he was killing people. The thoughts were too much. She poured herself a glass of wine, switched on the television, switched it off, poured another glass of wine. A knock at the door. Was it him? Was it the man she had given herself to as a teenager, the father of her child? What would she say? What would she do?

The knocking continued. Gwen got up from her chair. She knew instantly that she had drunk almost a full bottle of wine and that she was lightheaded.

Opening the door, she could see that it wasn't either of her husbands, it was her daughter. 'Mother, what have you been doing?'

'I've just had a drink.'

'A few drinks.' Sally walked to the kitchen and put on the kettle.

When she returned, carrying two coffees, one with milk, the other black, her mother was curled up in a foetal position in one of the chairs. 'Why?' her mother said repeatedly.

Sally had only come to see her mother, as she was troubled as well. She had intended to keep the meeting with her father a secret, but with her mother, she knew she could not. 'I've seen him,' she said.

'Where?' Gwen sat up and sipped her coffee.

'He approached Susie and me.'

'Did you recognise him?'

'Not at first, but it was him. It was hard. My father was dead, I've known that since I was a child, and there he is, in front of me.'

'What did he say?'

'He said he was sorry, and that he loves us.'

'The murders?'

'He said he had saved countless thousands by his actions. Susie liked him.'

'He held her?'

'No, but he gave her back her toy after she had dropped it. She held onto his finger, almost as if she knew who he was.'

'Did he tell you why he faked his death, and where he's been?'

'Not there. A policeman came over and disturbed us.'

'I want to see him,' Gwen said.

'We cannot tell anyone,' Sally said.

'Ed?'

'Especially not Ed.'

'Did he say that?'

'No, but there is animosity.'

'Why?'

'You married Ed, what do you think?'

'But your father was dead.'

'They wanted to use dad's research for something else.'

'And your stepfather may be involved?'

'I hope not, but it's best to hear from my father first.'

'We should tell the police.'

'To hell with the police, mother. He's my father, your husband. We owe him our confidence, at least for now.'

'You're right. If you see him again, let him know that I want to see him.'

It's complicated, isn't it?'

'Impossible, that's what it is. Where will it all end? Gwen asked.

'Badly, that's for sure, but what else can we do?'

'Nothing. We must continue, hoping for the best, expecting the worst.'

***

Malcolm Woolston was aware that his daughter had visited her mother. He knew that his ability to blend in was remarkable. A man wearing overalls and a hard hat, not uncommon in an area where every other house seemed to be involved in renovations.

He had wanted to knock on the door and go in, but he had seen the police car cruising slowly past, and besides, he did not know what Gwen's reaction would be, and whether he should meet her again. He knew that he wanted to throw his arms around her and to make love to her, but would that be possible, should he even consider it? Both had regarded marriage as exclusive, but now she was married to another, and he had been dead to her for years.

It was late afternoon before Sally left her mother's house. Woolston followed at a discreet distance. He waited until she was inside her own home before he left. He did not know why he had followed her; he certainly had no intention of contacting her that day. How many times had he followed her home in the past? He'd helped her on one or two occasions, even thrashing one man who had made her unhappy, and now she was unhappy again, and he was confusing the situation.

If those who had wronged him knew he had been in contact with Sally, his family would be used as levers, but how could he protect them? His decision to return to the real world and to deal with those who had dealt with him came with its attendant disadvantages: the risks to his family.

And Ed Barrow was carrying on with Sue Christie, and his wife did not know. Should he tell her? Should he tell her why he had returned? Would she understand? She had always been a stickler for the concepts of right and wrong. She would never understand that he had killed for a reason, although his daughter had; but then, she was more like him.

Woolston considered the way forward. If he announced what he knew to the media, they would not believe him. It may generate debate, but what use would that be? Officially the government would agree that there needed to be tighter controls on research and its misappropriation for illegal purposes, and that the government should not be involved in selling weapons to nations that had an unenviable human rights record, but those assurances had been given to him before, and then what had happened? Nothing. Just empty words flowing out into the ether.

He needed to protect his family; he needed help.

'Detective Chief Inspector Cook, this is Malcolm Woolston.'

'Mr Woolston, we have been looking for you,' Isaac said. 'How did you contact me?'

'Please tell Bridget Halloran not to trace this call.'

'How do you know the names of my staff?'

'Let us not fool ourselves here. You are aware of my academic achievements.'

'Yes, and what you have done since you've returned.'

'We can talk now, or I will phone back later.'

Isaac signalled to Bridget to stop trying to access the originating location of the call. Larry came into Isaac's office. 'DI Hill is here as well. Is that acceptable?'

'Yes. Please listen. Over eleven years ago, I was a research scientist at a government department in London. You've visited it, so I don't need to repeat the address.'

'That's true.'

'I, along with others, was working on a project to generate vast quantities of low-cost energy.'

'This we know.'

'What do you suspect?'

'That there was a plan to use it for non-peaceful purposes.'

'Who told you?'

'Helen Toogood.'

'Is she safe?'

'From me she is, and there's no way that she will be able to solve the problem. No one will harm her?' Woolston said.

'What about Ed Barrow?'

'We'll come to him in a while. There is a problem with the final solution that only I can solve. Some people will stop at nothing to force me to give them that solution.'

'Are you sure? This is England, we have rules and regulations.'

'Idealistic, I'll grant you. This country is as sadistic as any other given the opportunity, and those who have died, who must die, are not worthy of compassion.'

'George Arbuthnot?'

'The man was there when I was tortured, even took part. I had told Ed Barrow that I would not let my work be used for violent means.'

'And Barrow told others?'

'Yes.'

'Why?'

'Self-preservation, financial aggrandisement, power.'

'You've mentioned torture.'

'They tortured me. Do you want me to describe what happened?'

'The basics.'

'Harold Hutton was there and Ed Barrow was behind the scenes. I refused to give them what they wanted. Arbuthnot and his partner beat me for almost two weeks, sleep deprivation, electric shocks, the works.'

'Why was it so important?'

'I knew what they wanted to do. They wanted to take what I had and weaponise it. Then they would sell it to the highest bidder.'

'Government-sanctioned?'

'With the military, yes.'

'And now Ed Barrow is married to your wife. Why were you living on the street for eleven years?'

'I could protect my wife and daughter. They'll not hesitate to use them to get to me.'

'Is your research still relevant.'

'More so. The world is volatile. Rogue nations will pay plenty.'

'And the government could be involved?'

'Have you had any dealings with the government?' Woolston asked. 'What do you think?'

'I trust in the government,' Isaac said.

'Clichéd response. You know them as well as I do.'

'Are you willing to come in? It will go better at your trial.'

'There'll be no trial. They'll capture me, force me to work for them, or else they'll kill me.'

'How can they force you?'

'They have leverage, they would use Gwen and Sally, even my granddaughter.'

'They could have done that before.'

'I had died by then.'

'But this time you'll be alive.'

'Exactly, and it's possible I won't even be in this country. I'm damned whatever I do. I'm sorry about Bob Robertson. He shouldn't have let them know.'

'He didn't do it on purpose,' Isaac said.

'That's as maybe. I acted irrationally, I won't again.'

'Are there others that need to die?'

'Yes. Once I've dealt with them, then I will disappear.'

'Where to?'

'This time I won't be faking my death. Whatever happens, please protect my family.'

The phone went dead.

Isaac turned to look at Larry. He shook his head in disbelief.

***

Sue Christie often walked the three miles from her office to the flat she had purchased twenty years previously. The woman was at peace with the world, the first time for several weeks, the first evening that she and Ed had made love in his office since Malcolm Woolston had returned. She smiled at the thought of it.

She knew that she was a sensitive woman and that she should have married her lover when he had asked her the first time, and then all this nonsense with his marrying Gwen would not have occurred. Although, sensitive as she was, she was also fiercely independent, and an evening at home on her own with no one to talk to, no one to argue with, no one to make love to, suited her fine. Marriage she knew, came with responsibilities, none of which she cared for.

Ed had always treated her well, kept her satisfied, and then there was another man that she knew. She belonged to a generation where the men preferred the occasional dalliance, and some women, especially her, were able to accommodate them.

It was getting late in the evening as she crossed the road near to her place when a man grabbed her. 'Sue, we need to talk.'

Sue Christie looked up at the man holding her. A street light shone onto his face. 'Malcolm,' she exclaimed, fear gripping her.

'Don't worry. I'll not harm you.'

Sue remembered a kind man when they had all been friends, but this was someone from the past, someone who had been dead. She was frightened. 'Let me go. I've done nothing.'

'Apart from screwing Ed behind my wife's back.'

'That's only sex, nothing more, and besides, you've been dead for eleven years. Why are you here now?'

'Unfinished business, you know that. We'll talk inside your place.'

Sue fiddled in her handbag, attempting to find her phone. 'Don't try,' Woolston said.

'You've killed people.'

'People who deserved to die. Did you know about Arbuthnot, what he did to me?'

'Not really.'

The two walked towards the entrance to the block of flats where Sue lived. Woolston was holding the woman's arm firmly. 'Pretend that we're good friends.'

'We were once.'

'A long time ago.'

Once inside the main entrance to the block of flats, Woolston eased his grip. Sue made an attempt to bolt for the safety of her flat. 'I'll not harm you. That's my promise,' he said.

Realising that she had no option, she acquiesced and let him into her flat. 'Coffee?' she said.

'Yes, please. And don't try to make a phone call. We need to talk first.'

Sue looked at the man, could see that he had aged, but apart from that, she had to admit that he looked fine. Even with his lack of hair and the baseball cap that he wore, she would have recognised him.

'Why are you here?'

'There are files in the office that I want.'

'Why would I give them to you? And what files?'

'They're hidden.'

'Where?'

'I need your assurance that you'll help first.'

'Why would I help?'

'Because you have a mother.'

Sue Christie jumped up in alarm. 'You're mad.'

'Not mad, just determined. The moment I leave here, you'll be on the phone to Ed.'

'But my mother?'

'Your mother is the last resort to force your assistance. You'll be my first target.'

'But I've done nothing wrong.'

'Don't play the little Miss Innocent with me. You knew what Ed was up to, you knew about Arbuthnot and Hutton and how they treated me. Were you in for a cut of the profits?'

'What if I was? Life's difficult; it's dog eat dog out there. You and Gwen may have been idealistic, but the real world's not like that. You must know that now.'

'After eating out of rubbish bins, sleeping under bridges, yes, I know.'

'But why? What was the point of it all? You could have been living a great life with Gwen and Sally. Was it all worth it?'

'Would I act differently if I had my time over?'

'Yes.'

'Probably, but that's history now. I must complete what I started out to do.'

'And what is that?'

'I must not allow my research to fall into the wrong hands.'

'But they were British hands. Surely you can trust our government, our military, to do the right thing.'

'The government that sells weapons to third world countries to use against their own people?'

'Malcolm, it appears that all these years have not made you any smarter. Ed was right; you're mad.'

'I know my condition. I know what I was, what I have become. My only sanity is seeing this through.'

'And what about Gwen and Sally? Have you considered them?'

'They are safe as long as I have those files.'

'I won't help you. I have my convictions as well. I believe in what we are doing, and if your research is used for non-peaceful purposes, then so be it.'

Woolston looked around the flat. He had to admit that it still looked good, and that Sue, even though she was older, was still an attractive woman. He had fancied her back then, he still fancied her. He knew that she'd probably be available to him if he wanted her, but he did not intend to take advantage. He still harboured hope that he could reunite with Gwen, even if for only the one time. Sue, he knew, was complicit in what had happened. 'I'm sorry, but you will help me.'

'Would you harm my mother?'

'I killed Liz Hardcastle. What do you think?'

'She fell in front of a train. It was early morning; she was jostled by the crowd.'

'I did not want to kill Liz, but she was the smartest person in the department. The only person capable of understanding the problems.'

'Malcolm, you're not the person that Ed and I considered as a friend.'

'That isn't important. I have two objectives: one, to protect my family, and, two, to indefinitely delay further research on the project.'

'It is a government project.'

'You know what I mean.'

Sue Christie did not say it, but, yes, he was right. She did know about his work and the fact that others, including Ed, had been behind the scenes, discussing ways to commercialise a weapon that a department in another part of London was working on. In one place, Malcolm and his team were working on low-cost energy; in another, another team were taking the results and creating a weapon that once commissioned would be able to take that energy and destroy vast tracts of land and millions of people.

'Where is this file?'

'Phone your mother first. Check if she spoke to a man today about painting her house.'

'You bastard. You'd harm my mother?'

'I will do whatever is necessary. Phone your mother now.'

Sue picked up the phone and dialled. A short conversation and she ended the call.

'I've no option, have I?'

'None at all. I apologise, but from now on, I will do what is necessary.'

'They'll grab Gwen and Sally.'

'Not if I have that file. And don't think about letting Ed know of our conversation, and don't try moving your mother. Any action against me, and I'll deal with whoever, including your mother, as well as your two sisters. Believe me, I've done my homework.'

'When do you want this file?'

'Twenty-four hours.'

'You've not told me where it is.'

'I'll contact you in due course.'

Chapter 20

Woolston had not enjoyed threatening Sue. Her mother was innocent of all crimes, but he needed leverage. The files were well hidden, and someone smart may have been able to decipher them if they were found. Liz Hardcastle could have probably, although she had not known where the files were, only of their existence.

Of all the people that had died, he regretted her death more than any other. They had worked together for two years and had formed a firm friendship at work, but never outside. Her husband, he knew, was into bird watching and the outdoor life. Liz had confided that she'd rather stay at home and potter around the house, but with her husband, every Saturday it was early in the car and off to another forest or marsh or wherever birds congregate. She had become his walking encyclopaedia on their names, their Latin names as well.

He remembered her smiling, inquisitive face, her constant need to understand his work, able to correct him when he made the occasional mistake. Apart from Gwen, he had to admit that he had liked her a lot. They both knew, he and Liz, that in different circumstances they would have been more than just work colleagues: he, the brilliant research mathematician and scientist, she, his intellectual equal. It had been her who had seen the potential of their work as a weapon; her who had inadvertently mentioned it to Ed Barrow, who had mentioned it to Hutton. Woolston shuddered at the chain of events that had resulted.

If only he hadn't taken Liz into his confidence, about how there was a possibility of stabilising the power generated so that maximum power, maximum destructive power could be gained.

Liz, idealistic as he was, had not deserved to die that day in the railway station, he knew that, but she did not have the determination to resist.

It had been six months after his death that he had made his decision. He had seen Arbuthnot around the research department, even drinking with Ed Barrow in a local pub, which could only mean one thing: they were about to apply pressure, or they already had, and it could only be on Liz.

The railway station was crowded, and even then people had started to give him a wide berth due to his appearance. As he jostled in that crowd, edging closer to Liz, he still questioned whether he had the right to terminate her life. He had killed no one at that time, other than one of those that had tortured him. He could see her reading a book, quietly minding her own business. The train came into view. It was an express and not stopping. He edged forward, almost felt like saying sorry. A gentle nudge with his elbow, and she was in front of the train and then under it. Woolston remembered backing away from the scene as the other people moved forward. The newspapers carried the story the next day of how Liz Hardcastle, a government employee, well respected by her work colleagues, loved by her husband, had been in an unfortunate accident. It was the one time in the eleven years that he had drunk alcohol, a cheap bottle of wine, to allow him some peace. Her death had troubled him for months afterwards.

***

Isaac Cook and the Homicide team at Challis Street realised that the three deaths so far were unlikely to be the last. Malcolm Woolston, now no longer referred to as Big Greg, had not been seen for several weeks. The patrols of Gwen Barrow's and her daughter's streets had declined in regularity, and the uniforms at their homes had been pulled out after seven days.

DCS Goddard had been hoping for an early arrest, but that was not happening, and Commissioner Davies was still hovering, waiting to make his move. Isaac knew that something had to be done, but what? The links had been established, and the research department was the key, as was Gwen Barrow. Isaac had noticed Barrow and his wife at a local restaurant one night, and he had to admit they looked happy enough.

'We're getting nowhere fast on this case,' Isaac said. It was a throwaway line, he knew that, but what else was there for him to say. Malcolm Woolston had been visible, and then he had disappeared.

'Maybe there's no more,' Wendy said.

'The man phoned me up, Larry was here. He did not sound as though he was about to stop, quite the opposite. He told us that there were others who needed to be dealt with and that he was concerned for the safety of his family.'

'The man was sane?' Wendy asked.

'What do you reckon? Larry said.

'It's always hard to tell with these people, but we've checked on him. A brilliant man, a lot of academic papers, one book on advanced mathematics, although I couldn't make any sense of it, and then he tells us a story about others who want to take his research and use it as a weapon. He sounded sane enough, but he was determined. We've come across these sorts of people before. Most of them appear sane, but...'

'As you say, the screw loose, the chink in their armour, and what is this man's chink?'

'His weakness is his family. If these people are as vicious as he says they are, they'll not hesitate to use them to get to him.'

'But they haven't,' Larry said.

'Not yet, and Woolston's widow is married to one of the guilty, according to him. That's probably their only protection.'

'And no trace on his phone call?' Wendy said.

'We're rehashing old ground here. That's known already.'

***

Sue Christie had acted innocently with Malcolm Woolston, confident that he had bought her 'poor innocent little me' attitude. She knew that he had been easy to deal with, the same as he had always been. Even all those years ago she had known that he fancied her, but he was old school, a believer in the sanctity of marriage, honouring vows, fidelity. She knew she was not; she knew what she needed to do.

Her first action was to move her mother to somewhere safe: easily arranged. After that, there was one sister living overseas, another in Cornwall. She would need to be contacted, and that offer of a trip abroad would be hers.

Malcolm had given her twenty-four hours from the time of their meeting, which meant he would be phoning her that very day, and now there were two police officers in the office; one, the good-looking black man, the other, white, going to pot with his beer belly. She knew she fancied the black DCI, but not in the office, and not that day. She was a voracious man-eater, she knew that, but now she had to save those she cared for, or at least her mother and her sister, who was about to leave the country for a two-week holiday.

She had strung Ed Barrow along for years, made him feel that she cared for him, which she had once, but now he was a convenient lay, and more importantly, the way to a significant amount of money. He may not have known all the players involved, but she certainly did. General Claude Smythe had expressed interest in the project from its conception. He knew what it was worth, and how to get the money. He and his brother, the secretary of state for defence, were both ex-lovers, both opportunistic.

It was not often she saw the general, but whenever she did, she made sure that he left her with a smile on his face. Now she would know where the missing information was, and how to smuggle it out of the building, making sure that Ed did not know. He was expendable, and if Gwen was to be the grieving widow for the second time, then so be it. She could not care less.

'Mr Barrow,' Isaac said. He looked at Sue Christie, could see the smile on her face. He assumed it was for him. He had to admit that he liked the look of her, but her reputation, especially with Barrow, made her cheap and not his type.

'He's not here. I don't expect to see him today.'

'Do you have any idea where he is?'

'Personal business, that's all I know. Finding out that his wife's first husband is alive must make it difficult for him and Gwen.'

'It probably does, but it's important that we see him today.'

'Have you tried his home, his phone?'

'We have.'

'I'll let him know that you want to see him if he comes in.'

The two police officers left the building. 'It's a good job you checked in the car park first,' Isaac said.

'The man's there. What are they up to?' Larry said.

***

'They've gone?' Barrow asked.

'For now. The situation is getting dangerous.'

'Your mother?'

'She's fine.'

'Your sister?'

'I've done what I can.'

'And Malcolm's phoning today?'

'That's what he said. Do you have your people ready?' Sue asked.

'If they see him they'll grab him.'

'He told me not to tell you.'

'He's still naïve. He never could read you.'

'Whereas you could?'

'Sue, I've never bought your charm, not totally. I know that you're playing this to your advantage. You'd knife me in the back the first opportunity you got.'

'You're smarter than Malcolm then. All he ever wanted to do was to lay me.'

'And he never did, not even now when you're available.'

155

'I was always available.'

Ed Barrow had the measure of the woman, the woman who had put him in contact with those who would take what Woolston had discovered. Their promise that there'd be enough money for all of them had been the reason that he had consented to allow Woolston to be subjected to savagery, and now the woman was admitting that she'd sell him out if the opportunity presented itself.

'Can I trust you?' Barrow said.

'I will do what is right.'

'That's not an answer.'

'It's the only one you'll get from me. Malcolm is after vengeance, he's quite mad, you know. He'll stop at nothing to secure what he wants. You know what you have to do.'

'Not Gwen.'

'You always knew this day would come.'

'I suppose so.'

***

Ed Barrow left the office soon after talking to Sue. He realised that she and those she was in contact with would not honour their agreement to leave his family alone. He knew he had to protect them. He needed Malcolm Woolston.

As he drove out of the car park, a police car pulled up in front of him. 'Mr Barrow, you're required down at the police station. Either you drive there, or you can come with us.'

Realising that there was no way out, Barrow drove to the police station, the police car following. Isaac had realised that his personal assistant's assertion that he was not in the office when he was could only mean one thing: he had something to hide. Isaac intended to find out what it was.

'Mr Barrow, you are here voluntarily,' Isaac said in the interview room at Challis Street. 'Do you require legal representation?'

'No. I was busy when you called at my office, that was all. I asked Sue to cover for me.'

'There are aspects of this case that we don't understand.'

'I've told you all that I know.'

'Are you aware that Malcolm Woolston phoned us?'

'No.'

'He was lucid. He explained that his research was being diverted from peaceful purposes.'

'He's an idealist. How can any man live on the street for years, and then come back and start murdering people? It doesn't make sense.'

'He's also worried that his family is at risk.'

'They're my family as well. His daughter has accepted me as her de facto father, you do realise this?'

'We are aware of the close personal relationship that you enjoy with the mother and daughter. It does not explain why Malcolm Woolston sees you as a threat. Mr Barrow, are you a threat? Were you one of those that allowed Malcolm Woolston to be subjected to violence? Were you one of those who watched while the man suffered? Would you allow his wife and daughter to be harmed if it was beneficial to you?'

'What are you trying to portray me as, some kind of monster? Where's the proof? I'm a mid-ranking civil servant doing his job to the best of his abilities. I'm not to blame if one of my former team members goes crazy, fakes his death, lives on the street, and then starts murdering people.'

'I agree that it seems unlikely,' Isaac said, 'but it doesn't solve the case. Granted that Woolston appears to be a strange character, and if we find him, he will be charged with murder, but he seems rational. Arbuthnot was a shady character. You've met him?'

'On one occasion in the office.' Barrow was glad that his conversation with Helen Toogood had revealed that she had identified him from a photo.

'You did not tell us that before. We'll forget your oversight for now. What was his interest in your department?'

'He came with Hutton.'

'Arbuthnot was involved in arms trading. Did you know that?'

'Not at the time.'

'And you are agreeable for your research to be used for weapons?'

'I don't have an issue with that. We work for the government. How they use our results is up to them. Just because Woolston had an issue is not my concern. The only issue is the protection of my family. The research can go to hell if they're threatened.'

Chapter 21

At 4 p.m. Sue Christie received a phone call. 'This evening, you will leave your office at 6 p.m. You will walk home down Bayswater Road. When you reach number 128, you will see a rubbish bin. You will put the files in there. Is that clear?'

'Malcolm, where are they?'

'In my laboratory in the far corner there is a loose floorboard. It is covered with carpet. You will remove the carpet and use a screwdriver or something flat to prise up the floorboard. Under it you will find a box wrapped in plastic.'

'After eleven years?'

'It is still there.'

'How do you know?'

'It is my job to know.'

Sue Christie realised that there was only one way he knew that the files were still there. 'You could have asked Helen,' she said.

'I want you to do it.'

'Why?'

'I want to know if I can trust you.'

'Very well, but this cloak and dagger routine is banal.'

'The alternatives are not.'

***

Malcolm Woolston sat calmly in his flat. He weighed up the situation so far. It was necessary to trust some people, dispose of others. If he had stayed hidden, then there would have been no need for the deaths, but he had seen the formulas on the computer at Robertson's hostel. Other countries were close to developing low-cost energy, and he could have given his country the leading role. It was about to be lost, so it was necessary to reveal what he had done to the scientific community, believing that there would be companies in his country of birth who would seize the opportunity to use what he had developed for peaceful purposes. He typed on the laptop the final paragraphs of his technical paper. He needed some way to present his results. Sue Christie had supplied him with the missing information, no doubt taking a copy first, but he did not need the files. And besides, they were the substitutes that Helen Toogood had put there for him. He owed the woman his eternal thanks for believing in him, even reluctantly understanding his actions, and importantly, exposing Sue Christie.

There was no doubt that Ed Barrow was guilty of crimes against him, as was Sue Christie. He wasn't sure who was the worst, but it appeared that the woman was the guiltier. He had always had his suspicions, even before he took to the street. She was always too available, too polite, and too willing to offer herself to him.

He had known that Gwen was sometimes jealous, but she always took him at his word, and besides Sue was with Ed, and they were always good friends. But he had caught Sue once looking through his notes, pretending to be curious, not that she would have understood what she was reading; few people would have.

He had followed Sue down Bayswater Road, seen her turn into Westbourne Street and enter the restaurant. He had even seen her kiss the man that she met on the cheek as they sat down. A familiar face, he knew who it was. He had not seen her hand over the files but assumed she had. It would take them two days before they realised that what she had given him was worthless; time enough to complete what was necessary, to publish his paper, and to protect his family. It was a calculated risk, he knew that, and he was gambling with the lives of his wife and his daughter and her child. It was a risk he had to take.

***

Isaac Cook had a time issue as well. Apart from the occasional flurry of activity, the Homicide department was not working hard. The all points warning was still out for Malcolm Woolston, the case for the prosecution was tight, but they had nothing more. There was only so much walking the street, conducting interviews, looking at CCTV that could be done. After the conversation with Ed Barrow: nothing.

The joint funeral of Harold Hutton and his wife had been attended by a number of politicians, including the prime minister. There had been speculation, even by the PM, about what the police were doing to resolve this tragedy.

DCS Goddard, after the obligatory blasting out from Commissioner Davies, felt the need to vent his spleen in his office, Isaac standing to attention to hear him out. 'What's going on here?' Isaac mentally counted down from three minutes, the time for his DCS to change from argumentative to responsive.

'We're working on the case.'

'This man can't be that hard to find. You sit there with your small team, even after I've told you to get more people.'

Two minutes to go, Isaac thought.

'We're utilising other stations in our hunt for him.'

'And he's walking around the area, phoning you up, killing whoever.'

'He's not killed anyone since Hutton.'

'Great. Is that something to be thankful for?'

One minute, Isaac thought.

'Not at all. We've followed everything by the book, left no stone unturned. We've interviewed his former colleagues, spoken to his wife and daughter.'

'You know what Davies wants?'

'His man in my seat.'

'Exactly. What can I say to hold him off?'

'Will he listen?'

'You know the man.'

'Whatever we say, he'll counteract with invective.'

161

'Christ's sake, Isaac, sit down,' Goddard said. Isaac knew that now they could hold a worthwhile discussion. 'Hutton was important. Davies is being pressured as well on this one, and he's right to criticise. The fact that the man is a blithering fool is neither here nor there. He's our boss. I can't ignore him.'

'That's understood, sir. We believe that Woolston has a legitimate reason for his actions.'

'Murder? Legitimate?'

'We ran into this with the Marjorie Frobisher case.'

'Government interference, distorting the truth?'

'It's not the same, at least not in its entirety. Woolston realised that the government, probably others, were going to use his research for non-ethical purposes. He couldn't agree, they tried to force it out of him, he disappeared.'

'Very commendable, no doubt, but now he's killing people.'

'Apart from Robertson, which he regretted, he has killed another two.'

'Why do we always get these cases? What's wrong with a straightforward domestic dispute. Every case you take on always has some unforeseen complication. And now you're saying that murder is justified.'

'That's not what I said. Woolston believed that Hutton and Arbuthnot deserved to die.'

'Any more on his list?'

'He said he wasn't finished.'

'Names?'

'He didn't give them. And If Woolston is right, and there are government officials involved, you know what can happen.'

'We've been forced to cease our investigations before, let a murderer walk free because of an official directive. This one could be the same.'

'Are you meaning that Woolston may get off?'

'I'm not sure yet, but if he has vital information and they get to him first, then it's always possible.'

'And I'm meant to tell Davies all this?'

'Unfortunately, you'll just have to take the heat and keep us on the case.'

'Isaac, I believe you have an easier job than me,' DCS Goddard said.

***

In one corner of the room was the computer that had been taken from Bob Robertson's hostel. In another, a group of men studied Malcolm Woolston's files.

'It doesn't make sense to me,' the first of the men said.

'Nor me,' the second said.

The group had been working on solving the problem that had confronted them for over ten years, and they were no nearer to perfecting the weapon. Each time they tried, all they were able to do was to generate a minor explosion, but it was nowhere near the intensity or with the directional control needed.

They had the best equipment, General Claude Smythe had ensured that, the best security, and certainly the most powerful computers, yet none of it was sufficient. What they needed was the man. Smythe was aware of that fact, he had been for many years, and now with the files, and Sue Christie firmly in his corner, and Woolston having made contact with her, he was certain that it would only be days before the man would be joining the team. He wouldn't enjoy it, nor the country he would be taken to, and his accommodation, while adequate, would be spartan, with bars on the windows and guards at the only door to the cell. And if the man resisted, then he had people who could be very persuasive.

All Smythe had to do was to keep a watch on the woman, and the man would come. Originally it had been a concerted effort with Hutton to secure the solution from the naïve Woolston, to convert his work into a weapon and then to sell it to whoever was willing to pay, but time had moved on. Hutton was dead, so was Arbuthnot, and the field was clear for the general and his brother to reap all the rewards.

Claude Smythe had no illusions about what he and his brother were. Their lives had been ones of privilege and service to the community, and although he was a general in Her Majesty's army and his brother was a senior politician, they had realised that Woolston had given them access to more than a draughty castle and a government pension. An academic had given them the key to infinite wealth, the chance to live like kings, and Sue Christie came as an extra benefit, if only he could convince her to join with him.

At sixty years, Claude Smythe knew that he should be acting his age, but with the woman in his bed, he had felt twenty years younger. They had first made love twelve years previously, and whereas he knew what she was, and that she slept around, he also knew that she was the ideal woman: loving, devious, and willing to do anything if it was to her benefit. Pretending to care about Ed Barrow after he had married Woolston's widow was one instance, seducing him another.

Smythe appreciated driven personalities, and even though Sue Christie could never be trusted, she'd make an attractive addition to his lifestyle and he'd make sure she was well supported. As for Ed Barrow, the man had served his purpose. He had kept the department functional, but he had found no one with the ability to conclude Woolston's work. A decision would need to be made in the near future, but first the files that Sue had supplied had to be checked.

He phoned Sue. 'Tonight?' he said.

'Later. I've got to deal with Ed Barrow first.'

'Thursday night?'

Sue Christie smiled. Two men, both reeled in hook, line, and sinker. She had always known her impact on men. It was not that she was the most beautiful woman, nor the one with the best figure. She knew her breasts were too small, her hips too large, but it was the complete package that men lusted after, and she knew how to work it. Not only did she have a general, but she also had Ed Barrow, and she'd seen Malcolm Woolston mentally undressing her in her flat the other night when he had forced his way in. She knew that with Woolston, she would have the trifecta.

164

Chapter 22

Helen Toogood walked into the patent office in London at 10 o'clock on a Friday morning. She registered a document in the names of Malcolm Woolston and Helen Toogood. At precisely 11 a.m. she made a phone call. 'I've done what you asked. Are you sure about this?'

'Your name is registered as well. Even if I cannot take advantage, then you can,' Woolston said knowing that the possibility existed of government intervention in the patents' office.'

'Surely our research belongs to the government?' Helen said.

'Once my technical paper has been published, they'll not be able to claim it. The ability to misuse it has been removed. Do you think they'll want to admit to my torture, the fact that Ed Barrow is involved with people of ill-repute, that Harold Hutton was a bastard, and that General Claude Smythe and his brother are involved in illegal arms dealings?'

'But you can never benefit.'

'I'm not important, my family is. I trust you to share the rewards with them.'

'I will. What will you do now?'

'There are a few loose ends.'

'Ed Barrow?'

'I'm uncertain about him. It would upset Gwen if he died.'

'Why didn't you tell me you were alive?'

'I wasn't certain that I was coming back.'

'Why did you?'

'I knew that Bob Robertson had alerted them to me. I had to act.'

The phone call ended. Helen Toogood, the only person Woolston knew he could trust, the person he had first contacted when he had returned from the dead, had done her part.

At 8 p.m. the door swung open at Sue Christie's flat and she walked in. 'Malcolm, what are you doing here?'

'You've sold out. I saw you with Smythe. Are you screwing him as well as Ed?'

'What's it to you?'

'Did you know what they did to me, all those years ago?'

'Yes. Ed said it was necessary.'

'Those files you gave Smythe are as worthless as you are.'

'You set me up?'

'I needed to know who I could trust.'

'Helen?'

'She has done her part. Now you must do yours.'

***

Isaac Cook received the phone call at 8 a.m. the next morning. It was not often that he spoke to self-confessed killers. Typically, they preferred to keep their deeds under wraps, but Malcolm Woolston needed to talk, to someone he hoped would understand. 'I had to do it,' Woolston said.

Isaac signalled to Bridget on the other side of the department. She came running. 'Woolston,' he mouthed to her. Bridget retreated to instigate a check on where the phone call was being made from.

'Don't bother,' Woolston said. 'Our phone conversation will not take long, and besides, it's untraceable. Now listen.'

'I'm listening.'

'Even if you do not understand, there are reasons why my original research must remain hidden. It is why I continue to remove people who jeopardise that wish.'

'And what about your wife and daughter? Don't you place them at risk?'

'That is why they need protection.'

'But we cannot guarantee total protection.'

'I will help to ensure they are safe. You have met Sue Christie?' Woolston asked.

'Yes, on a few occasions.'

'She was willing to sell out if the price was right.'

'And what are you going to do.'

'It has been dealt with.'

'How?'

'132 Craven Terrace, ground floor. I suggest you check it out.'

'What will we find?'

'Sue Christie.'

'Is she?'

'Dead. Yes, she's very dead. An attractive woman in her time, but I could not let her live.'

'This is madness. You kill people and then phone me up. What kind of person does that?'

'Someone who understands who he is dealing with.'

***

'The man's psychotic,' Isaac said as he stood in Sue Christie's flat, the signs of a struggle clearly visible. A cat sat in one corner of the room; some flowers in a vase. The body of the woman sprawled across the floor. She had been strangled, her legs kicking out in her panic. Until now Isaac had been willing to concede that Woolston may have had an obscure, but valid reason for disposing of people, at least in his mind. Not that it excused him, but there had been murder enquiries in the past where the politics of the country had conflicted with the truth, and where the politics had taken precedence.

The average man in the street held the begrudging belief that the political masters had the best interests of the people at heart, but neither Isaac Cook nor his department, and certainly not his DCS, believed in that totally. Isaac knew of three deaths in previous cases that were government-sanctioned and would never be solved. But now he could no longer grant the man the benefit of the doubt. Woolston, for all his postulating, was a murderer without conscience.

'You don't need me to tell you who the murderer is this time, do you?' Gordon Windsor, the crime scene examiner, asked.

'It's Woolston. I've no idea what the man is playing at. His wife and daughter are in plain view. He must realise the risk that he's placing them under.'

'And you always thought the man was rational.'

***

Malcolm Woolston sat in his flat. The nightmares that had plagued him before his time on the street were returning. He was losing his ability to rationalise between reality and fiction, his capacity to distinguish between right and wrong. Sue Christie's death had been right, he was sure of that. After all, he had seen her give Smythe the files, or had she? She had left the office that day, deposited the files in the bin that he had told her to, and then carried on to meet one of the two military men that he had seen Ed with all those years before.

He had liked Sue, yet he had killed her, but what had she done, what could she do? The knowledge they wanted still resided with him.

She had struggled, he remembered that. Why had he enjoyed taking her life, he did not know. Maybe it was a deviancy, a repressed sexual desire, to want the woman, yet knowing he couldn't have her. She had pleaded with him for her life, even would have let him make love to her in return, but what had he done? He had sucked the life from her and left. And now there were others that needed to die, and soon.

Ed was a certainty, but his wife had betrayed him, slept with another. Did she need to die as well? And what about his daughter? She had shown affection for Barrow, even allowed him to walk her down the aisle when it should have been his responsibility. How could she? He paced up and down the flat, feeling the walls pressing in on him, thinking thoughts, not sure if they had attempted to force the solution out of him or whether it had been a dream.

He knew that he needed help. He phoned the only person who would understand. 'DCI Cook, I am not sure,' Woolston said.

'You've murdered Sue Christie.'

'What if none of it is true? What if I only imagine it? Could it be that I spent all those years living rough because of madness?'

'No one deserved to die, you know that. Why don't you come into the police station and we can discuss it?'

'Not yet. I need to decide.'

'Decide what?'

'If what I believe is true or not.'

'How can you tell?'

'I will wait. Rest, that is what I need.'

***

Richard Goddard was not in a good mood, which did not surprise Isaac. He'd let him express his customary criticism, his self-recrimination as to why he had let DCI Cook continue with the investigation when obviously he was not up to it.

After a few minutes, Goddard calmed down. 'What's this that you're saying? That you believe that the man is psychotic and no longer rational?'

'It's a possibility.'

'What if he is? How does that affect the current situation? How do you think this reflects on the department, on me?'

'Badly, I suppose.'

'Dead right, it does. Are you saying that none of the reasons that he gives for murdering four people are correct, and that we're just dealing with a mad genius, is that it?'

'It's probable.'

'Then you'd better find out,' Goddard said.

***

Ed Barrow was in a panic. Everyone who was close to him was dead, including Sue Christie. He realised, on hearing the news of her death, that he had liked her more than he would admit to. They had been together in that office for fifteen years and lovers for nine of them. He remembered the last time they had made love, only two days earlier, and that she had been full of life, optimistic for the future. Now she was dead.

All those who had been involved when Woolston had been detained and tortured were dead, apart from him. It was clear that the man was tidying up loose ends, and that he, Ed Barrow, had lasted longer than the others, but he was still a target. Woolston had told him that over the phone that one time. Sue Christie should have been protected. The woman was neither naïve nor stupid, yet somehow Malcolm Woolston had managed to get into her flat.

And what was she killed for? She had not been involved with Woolston's treatment eleven years previously. She knew about it, he had told her, Ed realised that, but her reaction had not been agreeable. To her, it had all been too sordid, although a percentage of any deals that might be made was attractive to her. Ed Barrow knew one thing: he needed to protect himself. He needed his wife's assistance.

'You've heard about Sue?' he asked Gwen in the front room of the house they shared.

'Tragic. Was it Malcolm?'

'No doubt.'

'Then he will be after you as well.'

'Yes.'

'According to Sally, he was maltreated all those years ago. The reason he faked his death.'

Ed Barrow could see no way to avoid the truth, or at least some of it. 'Malcolm was idealistic, holding onto a belief in the goodness of man.'

'You knew about this?'

'Not immediately, but some powerful people wanted him to talk,' Ed said, knowing full well that he had lied.

'Did Sue?'

'Not at first.'

'You're lying, I know it. She was killed because she was involved, the same as you. What Malcolm told Sally is all true. Why did you marry me? To keep an eye on me in case Malcolm knocked on the door? Is that it? And don't lie. And don't give me that innocent boy look that you do when you've been screwing Sue.'

'But...'

'But nothing and don't deny it. It didn't worry me at the time, it won't now. You're a bastard, a charming bastard. I didn't want to be alone, and you were the nearest thing there was to Malcolm, and Sally adored you.'

Ed Barrow sat down, a look of disbelief on his face. Gwen, a woman who had adored her first husband, had seen through him from the very beginning. 'There is no reason for Sue's death,' he said.

'Whatever it is that you and she had cooked up, it was responsible for Malcolm faking his death, and then coming back and killing people. What is this great secret that forces a man such as him to behave in this manner? Are you going to tell me, or are you going to sit there whimpering? And there's no point crying to your mistress, she's dead, and no great loss to society. You two are total bastards, you know that.'

'I love you,' Ed said.

'Maybe you do, but Malcolm's out there on his own. The man may have had his faults, but he never cheated on me even when Sue was giving him the eye.'

'We need to work together on this. What if Malcolm comes for me?'

'Why would he? What is it that you and Sue were involved in?'

Ed wasn't sure what to say. Should he level with her and tell her what he knew, what the plan was, how it was going to make them all rich, Malcolm included, if he had played ball. 'I need to return to the office. It's complicated. We'll talk later,' he said as he left the house.

After he left, Gwen picked up her phone. 'Sally, I want to see your father.'

Chapter 23

Claude Smythe had enjoyed the time that he had spent with Sue Christie, the snatched weekends in the country away from his wife. As a general in the British Army, he had had her checked out. He knew about her men, about Ed Barrow and their clandestine affair. He also knew that she was devious and could not be trusted, and that her tolerance of him, a man past his prime, was not because of love, but because of a lust for money, and with his contacts, she could achieve that.

The thought of her lying dead in her flat did not concern him. He'd seen enough death in his lifetime, and a woman in her forties, even one such as Sue Christie, was not going to faze him. He had seen Barrow with Woolston's widow, and whereas he did not like the man, he had to admit that he had good taste in women.

His brother would not have been interested, even if he broached the subject, which he had no intention of doing. With Cameron, it was always business, and especially the business of foreign arms trading, illegally if possible.

'Arbuthnot could have brought this off, kept us out of it,' Cameron Smythe said.

'No point in speculating. Woolston killed him,' Claude said.

'Woolston's a nuisance. What are you doing to bring this man in?'

'We've some people undercover looking for him.'

'Who?'

'Leave that to me. You just keep the contacts open.'

'There's a facility where he can go when you find him.'

'In England?'

'As you've just said, leave it to me. We'll have him out of the country within hours.'

'One-way trip?'

'He'll not be coming back. They'll extract whatever they want, force him to complete the project, and then…'

'When he's outlived his usefulness, they'll rid themselves of him.'

'Bullet to the head, that sort of thing.'

'Nasty.'

'Does it concern you?'

'Not at all.'

'Then how will you flush out Woolston?'

'There's only one way.'

'You've got the people?'

'Once we agree.'

'Are we there yet?'

'The files he gave us were fake. It was just a ruse to flush out Sue Christie.'

'It worked.'

'He's working to a plan. If he knows about us, then we'll be in his line of fire.'

'For a self-proclaimed pacifist, he certainly has no issue with murder.'

'He's the same as all of them. If it's a noble cause, then anything is justified.'

'Is it a noble cause?'

'This project of low-cost energy? I suppose it is, but the alternative project is of more interest to us.'

***

Isaac brought the team together in Challis Street. Sue Christie's death had brought renewed focus on the Homicide department to find Malcolm Woolston.

'Woolston didn't kill her without reason,' Larry said.

'Woolston's told me that already. If she had sold out, as he claimed, then that means Ed Barrow has too.'

'That's never been a secret that Woolston intends to kill Barrow as well.'

'Is he the last on the list?' Wendy asked.

'We'll not know unless the man contacts us.'

Isaac's phone rang. 'There are people after me,' Woolston said.

'We are,' Isaac replied.

'It is important that these people do not catch me.'

'What do you mean?'

'They will force me to complete a weapon of immense destructive capability.'

'You could refuse.'

'That will not be possible.'

'Why?'

'They will threaten my family.'

'Why didn't you stay dead?' Isaac asked. 'Leave well alone?'

'I knew Bob Robertson's surfing the net would cause trouble. I had to pre-empt them.'

'What do you want us to do?'

'I want you to know in case anything happens to my family or to me.'

'We can't protect your family any more than we are now, and besides, if you surrender yourself to us at Challis Street, you'll be protected.'

'There is no protection there for me. I just wanted you to know.'

'Where will they take you?'

'You will never find me, they'll make sure of that.'

'We would continue to look. You are still a self-confessed murderer.'

'They will stop it, apply the Official Secrets Act.'

'We've been there before,' Isaac said.

'Then you know what I'm talking about.'

'Whether I do or not is immaterial. You have committed crimes, I'm a police officer. I have my duty to do.'

'They will not allow you.'

Yet again, Isaac had to admit, a bizarre phone call.

***

Gwen Barrow did not often travel to the centre of London. It was her first time there for some years, and the meeting in a hotel room close to Leicester Square was important.

As she entered through the swing doors of the hotel, a wave of nostalgia swept over her. It was where she and Malcolm had honeymooned. Even the room was the same.

She wasn't sure what to expect, not sure if she should have agreed, but Sally said it had been arranged, and it was important. Besides, there were questions unanswered. It had been eleven years since she had seen the man, not all of them bad, but now with Ed almost certainly involved in something nefarious, and Malcolm killing people, her relationship with her current husband was tenuous.

Ever since Malcolm had returned, she had not slept well, not wanting to see him, wanting to see him, and there he was standing in front of her as he opened the door. Gwen was not sure if she wanted to chastise him or hug him.

'A long time,' he said.

'I wasn't sure.'

'Hear me out.' Malcolm put his arms around his former wife and gave her a hug and a kiss on the cheek. She did not react.

'Why here?'

'I couldn't think of anywhere else that had pleasant memories.'

'You've not changed,'

'I'm older, less hair, but I suppose I'm still the same.'

'Sally said I had to come. I was in two minds.'

'She was right. It may be the only chance that we get to spend time together.'

'If you hadn't killed anyone.'

'Not even then. They'll not leave me alone.'

'They?'

'The government, the military, Ed.'

'He's been a good man to us,' Gwen said.

'He's involved.'

'But why Sue?'

'She had her fingers in too many pies.'

Gwen sat down on the bed. The man looked the same to her, a little older maybe, and where there should have been hair, there was none. The voice remained the same, the mannerisms. She was in their honeymoon suite, yet she felt she was with a stranger.

Ed had been there for them for the last eleven years, in truth a better father to Sally than the man standing in front of her, yet he had not been the father. And now, Malcolm Woolston was back in their lives. She had not known that Sally had a phone number for her father and that she had phoned him up after her mother's request.

Gwen was not sure what to expect, what she wanted from the meeting. Malcolm came forward, attempted to put his arms around her. She pulled back. 'It's been so long. I don't know if I can,' she said.

Malcolm, her resurrected husband, moved to the other side of the room and sat in a chair. 'I had to disappear.'

'I was wrong to come,' Gwen said.

'Then why?'

'I had to know.'

'That I'm alive?'

'If you are capable of murdering people. If I'm safe. If Sally and Susie are safe.'

'You have always been safe, but then you went and married Ed.'

'But you must have known.'

'Yes, but I was willing to concede that it was the best thing at the time.'

'And now?'

'On the street, it was so much easier, but then since I've returned, the situation is not clear. I'd always suspected Sue, and even Ed did not know of her duplicity.'

'But why is this so important? This talk of weapons makes no sense. The government is always trading with rogue nations, selling them arms, currying favours, especially if they have oil. What is so different with what you developed?'

'I needed to make a stand. To show them that someone still has ethics.'

'And leave us on our own? What ethics are those?'

'You should not have come.'

'I had to see you one more time.'

'Before what?'

'Before they take you. They will, you know that.'

'I cannot allow them to do that.'

'I'm asking you not to kill Ed.'

'Why? Do you love him? Can you forgive him for what he did to me?'

'He's important to us, and yes, I love him. Maybe it's not the same as with you, but he's been there for us, you haven't.'

'He was having an affair with Sue Christie.'

'I'd always suspected it. It upsets me to think about it, but I can forgive him for that; I cannot forgive you for killing Sue.'

'She would have sold out Ed or anyone who got in her way. I tested her. She was involved with Claude Smythe.'

'General Smythe?'

'And with his brother. The two are traitors. Their involvement is suspect, and not even Ed knows about them.'

Gwen realised that the man who had been her husband was delusional, seeing conspiracies when there were none, killing people for no reason, upsetting his family's lives. She pulled a gun from her handbag.

'What the hell?'

'I can't allow this to continue,' she said. 'If someone is after you or not, it does not matter. Whatever happens, they will not use us as a lever if you're dead.'

'You'd shoot me? What about Sally? What about our granddaughter?'

'You should have thought of that before. You should have remained dead. Our lives were fine before you came back.'

'I need to finish this,' Woolston said.

'It stops here.' Gwen pointed the gun and pulled the trigger.

Woolston was hit in the chest. Gwen ran over to him, tears streaming down her face. There was the sound of people running in the corridor after the noise of the gunshot.

'Gwen, leave,' Woolston said.

'I'm sorry. I had to.'

The door opened, two men and a woman stood there. 'What the...' the hotel manager said. 'Phone for an ambulance and the police.'

'Let her go,' Woolston said faintly.

'I can't do that. She's attempted to kill you.'

'She's my wife. I'll not press charges.'

'Charges? I don't think that applies, do you? A clear case of attempted murder from what I can see.'

Gwen sat close to her husband, cradling his head in her lap. 'I'm sorry.'

'You're right. The madness has to stop. I had wanted to stop it falling into the wrong hands, but now, maybe, it's not so important.'

***

Isaac Cook had despaired about how to deal with Malcolm Woolston and the murders he had committed, and now the man was at St Bartholomew's Hospital in West Smithfield in intensive care. And coupled with that, his wife, or at least his ex-wife, was under arrest, having been charged with his attempted murder.

Isaac and Larry made the trip to the hospital after receiving a phone call from Sergeant Hastings, the first police officer on the scene. At the hospital, they flashed their ID badges and proceeded to the emergency department. A doctor came out and spoke to them after they had been there for fifty minutes. 'Mr Woolston has been shot in the chest. There's some damage to one of his kidneys, but he will survive. He's a lucky man.'

'I doubt if he'll agree with you,' Isaac replied. Larry and Sergeant Hastings stood close by.

'When can we question him?' Larry asked.

'Not today. It's possible tomorrow, but he'll still be weak. Is it important?'

'Yes.'

'Sergeant Hastings,' Isaac asked after the doctor had left, 'did he say anything?'

'He was unconscious by the time we arrived. The medic stabilised him and then brought him here.'

'He'll need a uniform to guard him.'

'He's not going anywhere fast.'

'There's more to this case than you know. It's not only him getting out; it's also about preventing others getting in. His wife?'

'Down at the station.'

'We'll need to interview her.'

'No problem. She's been charged with murder.'

Chapter 24

Gwen Barrow was looking sorry for herself when she was led into the interview room. Ed Barrow was outside with Sally.

'We'll talk later,' Isaac said to the two of them as he walked through with Larry Hill.

'Mrs Barrow, you've been charged with attempted murder,' Isaac said, after dealing with the formalities.

'He had to die,' Gwen Barrow replied. 'I had to protect my family.'

'You could have told us where he was. We could have arrested him.'

'I needed to see him, to know whether he's sane or mad.'

'We need to know how you knew he would be in the hotel.'

'He phoned me.'

'We will be checking your phone records. If we find any inconsistencies, it will not be to your advantage.'

'Will he live?'

'According to the doctor, he will.'

'He had phoned Sally; she phoned me. I wanted to see him after he killed Sue Christie.'

'Why?'

'He was my husband. I needed to know.'

'What did he say?'

'Yes, he admitted to killing her, as well as the others. He would have told me more, but I needed to complete my task.'

'It was premeditated?'

'He intended to kill Ed.'

'What were his reasons?'

'He thinks he and Sue had sold him out.'

'Had they?'

'Probably not, but with Ed, you can't be sure.'

'What do you mean?'

'They were having an affair.'

'We suspected that. Do you have proof?'

'A woman doesn't need proof, she knows.'

'Did your daughter know your plans?'

'No.'

Isaac realised that the interview was not going well for Gwen Barrow. The woman was guilty, Malcolm Woolston was in the hospital, and the case was effectively closed. Although Woolston's motives may have been idealistic, he had still committed murder.

'Was this the first contact you had with your ex-husband?'

'Yes.'

'And Sally?'

'You'll have to ask her.'

'We'd like to hear from you first.'

'Sally had met him in the park.'

Isaac realised that the two women were guilty of not informing the police about Woolston, but it was probably not enforceable, and under the circumstances a conviction was unlikely.

'Please tell Malcolm that I'm sorry,' Gwen Barrow said.

***

DCS Goddard phoned not long after Isaac and Larry left the interview room. 'Case is wrapped up, a definite conviction,' he said.

'I suppose you're right,' Isaac said. 'The man's not going anywhere, and his wife has admitted to attempted murder, but why?'

'Isaac, you do this every time. Let sleeping dogs lie. If there's something else it's not our business. Just make sure the case for the prosecution is watertight.'

'There's more.'

'You and your department have been mandated to solve homicides. And that's what you've done. If Woolston is mad or whether they were justifiable killings, according to him, you've done your job. Just wrap this up and leave well alone.'

***

Sally had been distraught on learning that one of her parents, a self-confessed murderer, was in intensive care in a hospital and the other, her mother, had been charged with attempted murder. In spite of the circumstances of her father's apparent suicide many years previously, she had led an untroubled life, apart from the usual rebelliousness during her teenage years. And now she had the conflict of divided loyalties for two people that she loved, and the need to recognise the fact that both were under arrest, and neither were likely to be free to walk the streets for a very long time, if ever.

'Why, mother?' Sally asked her in a secure room at Challis Street.

'He intended to kill Ed. I had to stop him.'

'But shooting my father?'

The two women were sitting on the small, uncomfortable bed. Neither woman was able to deal with the other. Gwen wanted her daughter to leave. If Malcolm had died, it would have been better for all concerned, but it appeared that he would live, which only complicated the situation.

'He killed Sue Christie, did you know that?'

'They told me upstairs.'

'I just wanted it to stop. Your father was never mad, but what he did, disappearing like that, then returning to blight our lives.'

'Did he explain why?'

'He blames Ed, and he said Sue was worse. Whatever it is, it had to stop. Can't you see that?'

'Not at all. I've two parents, both murderers. How do you think this will affect Susie as she grows up, knowing that her grandparents are criminals?'

The two women held hands, not sure what else to say. After ten minutes, Sally left, leaving her mother lying on the bed, her face pressed into the pillow.

'What did she say?' Ed asked Sally on her return upstairs. He had grabbed a coffee out of an automatic vending machine. He realised the seriousness of the situation with regards to Gwen, a woman he cared about, and Malcolm, who had been a friend but was now a social leper. The man had killed Sue Christie, and whereas he had not been upset over the deaths of Arbuthnot and Hutton, he was of the woman that he had once loved, once proposed marriage to, made love to on a weekly basis.

Sure, he had known that she had been a smart woman, always playing one man off against another, using her beguiling nature to seduce and discard as she wanted, but she had been loyal to him, even when Malcolm had first been waylaid by Arbuthnot.

He remembered that she had been a softer soul then, concerned that what was happening to a friend in a remote location was wrong. It had taken all his charms to convince her of the necessity, but then he came to know that her concern was an affectation and that what convinced her was the potential money involved.

And then there was her and other men. He knew about the general, a man who should have known better, although he could not blame the old fool. The man and his brother were men who portrayed respectability, the best of British, yet they were always willing to strike a deal with anyone, if it was to the country's benefit or theirs.

Sally felt guilt in that she had set up the meeting between her parents, hoping that it would resolve issues, not knowing that her mother, the one constant in her life, was contemplating a violent action. And now all she had was Ed, but he wasn't her real father. That man was lying in a hospital bed.

'I'd like to see my father,' Sally said to Isaac when he spoke to her at the station.

'I'll need a statement first as to how you knew how to contact your father.'

'And then?'

'I'll see what can be arranged.'

Isaac looked over at Ed Barrow. 'Did you know about this?'

'Not at all. It's a mess.'

'Murder always is. Invariably it's the innocent who suffer the most.'

'That's us,' Barrow said.

Sally at least, Isaac thought. He still had his doubts about Barrow.

***

Over the course of a few days, Malcolm Woolston's condition continued to improve. He had been formally charged with the murders of Bob Robertson, Sue Christie, Harold Hutton, and George Arbuthnot. As he had freely admitted to their slayings, he had no difficulty in signing a confession to that effect. Richard Goddard was delighted, and had been the first to phone Commissioner Davies with the good news. Also, Gwen Barrow had been charged and transferred out to a prison pending trial, bail refused.

Isaac had a nagging feeling that all was not right. He had wrapped up the case, dealt with the case for the prosecution, collated all the evidence, interviewed all the people intimately involved and those on the periphery.

'What is it?' Larry asked. He had seen his DCI sitting in his chair, eyes closed, thinking.

'We still don't understand why.'

'Is it important?'

'Probably not, but Woolston's still in the hospital, and he shows no guilt for his actions.'

'It's not for us to psychoanalyse the man.'

'I agree. And then his former wife attempts to kill him. A woman with no history of criminal behaviour whatsoever.'

'DCS Goddard would tell you to leave well alone and just take the credit for wrapping up another investigation.'

'He's right, I know that.'

'Then, with respect, sir, drop it.'

'What causes a man to leave his family? You've met Gwen Barrow and their daughter?'

'Good people, so is the father, apart from what he's done.'

'Did we investigate Woolston's project?'

'We're Homicide. Is it relevant?'

'Not in itself, but Woolston thought it was, otherwise he wouldn't have put himself through eleven years of purgatory. The man had enjoyed the good life, and then he's out on the street with all its deprivations.'

'Personally, I think the man just lost it.'

'Maybe you're right. Let's wrap up the case and take a break for a few days until some other idiot decides to kill someone else.'

'A few days? More like a few hours judging by our luck.'

A sense of calm reigned in the Homicide department. Final interviews had been concluded with Ed Barrow, Helen Toogood, and Sally. Malcolm Woolston, his condition improving, remained in the hospital, although no longer in intensive care, and he was back on his feet. He was the only person that maintained a level of agitation. Outside his private room at the hospital, the uniforms were stationed on an eight-hour rotating basis, and there was a secure and barred door that isolated the wing from the general hospital. Isaac kept in contact with the man, but he had little to say, other than it wasn't over yet. Woolston kept reaffirming that his wife was innocent of all crimes and should be released.

Isaac thought that under the circumstances a lenient charge may give her a reduced sentence, possibly no time in prison, but it would be exceptional. Still, if asked to provide evidence, he knew that he would make a plea for leniency based on the woman's cooperation, and the desire to save her husband,

Ed. There were two facts that did not gel: why would Malcolm Woolston want to kill Ed Barrow and why had he killed Sue Christie?

***

For once Ed Barrow found himself without a job. As the department's research director, he had been given the sack. It had come quickly after the death of Sue Christie and the arrest of Malcolm Woolston. Barrow could see the hand of influence and power behind the scenes. He knew how it worked, having used it when Malcolm Woolston had refused to reveal the final solution to his research project.

Then it had been easy. Harold Hutton had counselled him on what was required after he had informed him, but who was calling the shots now? Barrow didn't know, and it concerned him. He had made a few phone calls, received bland responses, or maybe he had called the wrong people.

Barrow was desperate. Without any support mechanism in place, and in a trial, proof that Malcolm Woolston had been tortured, the questions would come back on him, and what did he have? Nothing. No written record, no recorded conversations, and the only persons who could corroborate his story were all dead, killed by Woolston.

Ed Barrow travelled to where his wife was being held. He found her in a conciliatory mood. 'Malcolm's going to live,' she said.

'That's not what you intended.'

'What were you up to? What caused Malcolm to do what he did?'

Both of them realised that whatever happened, their marriage was doomed.

'The man was idealistic. He brought this on himself.'

'He always was, you know that. Did you have him tortured?'

'I knew about it, but it was not my idea. I was placed in a dilemma. One of those decisions in life which cannot be defined by a simple yes or no.'

'And now I'm in jail, charged with murder.'

'Life takes unknown directions. It's not over yet.'

'What do you mean?'

'The project that Malcolm was working on is still valid.'

'They'll make him continue?'

'He'll either agree, or they'll force him.'

'Can they?'

'They know his Achilles' heel.'

'Sally and me?'

'Yes.'

'Would they?'

'Those bastards will do anything.'

'Do you know who they are?'

'I have my suspicions.'

'Then you'd better contact them.'

'I have already.'

***

Two men met. Two men who had little in common apart from the fact that both were ex-lovers of Sue Christie. Claude Smythe was British Army, the son of a duke. Ed Barrow was a civil servant, the son of a bus driver and educated at the local grammar school, not at Eton.

'Barrow, you know what's needed,' Smythe said. There was to be no friendly conversation this time. Smythe had the irritating habit of referring to his social inferiors by their surnames.

'You know what I require?'

'It's already been agreed.'

'In writing? Barrow asked.

'No one will claim responsibility if this goes wrong.'

Ed Barrow could see that he had to trust the man. He did not like Smythe, despised him in many ways. His father had been working class and a decent, hardworking individual who had never cheated on his taxes, helped the old dears on and off his bus. Smythe, Barrow knew, would help no one.

The conversation had been brief, a handshake on their meeting, another on leaving. Barrow knew that he was placing his trust in a man he did not like, but he had no option.

Two days later, as Malcolm Woolston hobbled down the corridor outside his room at the hospital, an order came through signed by Commissioner Davies for his immediate release. Another two hours and Woolston stood on the street in the company of two men dressed in suits. 'Ed Barrow?' he asked.

'We're just the delivery men,' the shorter of the two said.

'Where are you taking me?'

'You'll see.'

A vehicle drew up alongside, its windows tinted. Once inside, and with Woolston pinned between the two men on the back seat, one of them took out a syringe from his pocket and injected him in the neck.

'How long will he sleep?' the other one asked.

'Long enough.'

***

The first Isaac and his team heard of the events at the hospital was a phone call thirty minutes later.

'They've released Woolston,' Richard Goddard said.

'Who's they?' Isaac asked.

'Davies received a directive.'

'And he released the man? He may be the commissioner of the Met but he doesn't have the authority.'

'He had no option.'

'Protecting his job, is that it?'

'Isaac, you may well be upset, so am I, but we all have someone we report to.'

'Even Davies?'

'We've been there before. You know how it works.'

'Security of the state?'

'They're the government. We do what we're told.'

Isaac called in the team to his office. 'They've released Malcolm Woolston.'

'All charges dropped?' Isaac asked his DCS on the phone.

'The charges still apply.'

'Gwen Barrow?'

'There'll be a trial.'

'A whitewash?'

'What do you think?'

***

Isaac and Larry left the office soon after their DCS's phone call. They found Ed Barrow at his house. 'Were you involved?' Isaac asked.

Barrow sat calmly on a chair. He fiddled with his smartphone. Isaac wanted to pick it up and to throw it out of the window, as angry as he was.

'Woolston?' Barrow said, pretending not to know.

'Where is he?'

'I don't know. He's gone, that's all I know.'

'You've sold out.'

'Sold out to who and what?'

'Those who wanted him.'

'It's not a matter that I can talk about.'

'Why?'

'Official Secrets Act. You've heard of it.'

'I've heard of it. What did they offer you? A salary increase, a promotion.'

'I didn't do it for that.'

'Then for what?'

'My family, that's who.'

'Your wife is still in jail.'

'She is safe, as is Sally and her child. That's what Malcolm wanted all along. I've done what he couldn't.'

Within one week Gwen Barrow was released on bail; six weeks later the charge against her was dropped.

In another country, in a secure establishment, Malcolm Woolston worked at the project he had tried to avoid for so many years. He was aware of the penalty for failure to complete it, the penalty for any attempt on his part to delay it.

'Malcolm, they're safe. That's all that's important,' Ed said to him in the small room that constituted Woolston's living quarters.

Woolston nodded his head weakly, knowing that it had all been in vain. They would have their weapon, and he would never see England or his family again.

The End

ALSO BY THE AUTHOR

Death Unholy – A DI Tremayne Thriller

All that remained were the man's two legs and a chair full of greasy and fetid ash. Little did DI Keith Tremayne know that it was the beginning of a journey into the murky world of paganism and its ancient rituals. And it was going to get very dangerous.

'Do you believe in spontaneous human combustion?' Detective Inspector Keith Tremayne asked.

'Not me. I've read about it. Who hasn't?' Sergeant Clare Yarwood answered.

I haven't,' Tremayne replied, which did not surprise his young sergeant. In the months they had been working together, she had come to realise that he was a man who had little interest in the world. When he had a cigarette in his mouth, a beer in his hand, and a murder to solve he was about the happiest she ever saw him. He could hardly be regarded as one of life's sociable people. And as for reading? The most he managed was an occasional police report or an early morning newspaper, turning first to the back pages for the racing results.

Murder in Little Venice – A DCI Cook Thriller

A dismembered corpse floats in the canal in Little Venice, an upmarket tourist haven in London. Its identity is unknown, but what is its significance?

DCI Isaac Cook is baffled about why it's there. Is it gang-related, or is it something more?

Whatever the reason, it's clearly a warning, and Isaac and his team are sure it's not the last body that they'll have to deal with.

Murder is only a Number – A DCI Cook Thriller

Before she left she carved a number in blood on his chest. But why the number 2, if this was her first murder?

The woman prowls the streets of London. Her targets are men who have wronged her. Or have they? And why is she keeping count?

DCI Cook and his team finally know who she is, but not before she's murdered four men. The whole team are looking for her, but the woman keeps disappearing in plain sight. The pressure's on to stop her, but she's always one step ahead.

And this time, DCS Goddard can't protect his protégé, Isaac Cook, from the wrath of the new commissioner at the Met.

Murder House – A DCI Cook Thriller

A corpse in the fireplace of an old house. It's been there for thirty years, but who is it?

It's clearly murder, but who is the victim and what connection does the body have to the previous owners of the house. What is the motive? And why is the body in a fireplace? It was bound to be discovered eventually but was that what the murderer wanted? The main suspects are all old and dying, or already dead.

Isaac Cook and his team have their work cut out trying to put the pieces together. Those who know are not talking because of an old-fashioned belief that a family's dirty laundry should not be aired in public, and certainly not to a policeman – even if that means the murderer is never brought to justice!

Murder is a Tricky Business – A DCI Cook Thriller

A television actress is missing, and DCI Isaac Cook, the Senior Investigation Officer of the Murder Investigation Team at Challis Street Police Station in London, is searching for her.

Why has he been taken away from more important crimes to search for the woman? It's not the first time she's gone missing, so why does everyone assume she's been murdered?

There's a secret, that much is certain, but who knows it? The missing woman? The executive producer? His eavesdropping assistant? Or the actor who portrayed her fictional brother in the TV soap opera?

Murder Without Reason – A DCI Cook Thriller

DCI Cook faces his greatest challenge. The Islamic State is waging war in England, and they are winning.

Not only does Isaac Cook have to contend with finding the perpetrators, but he is also being forced to commit actions contrary to his mandate as a police officer.

And then there is Anne Argento, the prime minister's deputy. The prime minister has shown himself to be a pacifist and is not up to the task. She needs to take his job if the country is to fight back against the Islamists.

Vane and Martin have provided the solution. Will DCI Cook and Anne Argento be willing to follow it through? Are they able to act for the good of England, knowing that a criminal and murderous action is about to take place? Do they have any option?

The Haberman Virus

A remote and isolated village in the Hindu Kush mountain range in North Eastern Afghanistan is wiped out by a virus unlike any seen before.

A mysterious visitor clad in a space suit checks his handiwork, a female American doctor succumbs to the disease, and the woman sent to trap the person responsible falls in love with him – the man who would cause the deaths of millions.

Hostage of Islam

Three are to die at the Mission in Nigeria: the pastor and his wife in a blazing chapel; another gunned down while trying to defend them from the Islamist fighters.

Kate McDonald, an American, grieving over her boyfriend's death and Helen Campbell, whose life had been troubled by drugs and prostitution, are taken by the attackers.

Kate is sold to a slave trader who intends to sell her virginity to an Arab Prince. Helen, to ensure their survival, gives herself to the murderer of her friends.

Malika's Revenge

Malika, a drug-addicted prostitute, waits in a smugglers' village for the next Afghan tribesman or Tajik gangster to pay her price, a few scraps of heroin.

Yusup Baroyev, a drug lord, enjoys a lifestyle many would envy. An Afghan warlord sees the resurgence of the Taliban. A Russian white-collar criminal portrays himself as a good and honest citizen in Moscow.

All of them are linked in an audacious plan to increase the quantity of heroin shipped out of Afghanistan and into Russia and ultimately the West.

Some will succeed, some will die, some will be rescued from their plight and others will rue the day they became involved.

ABOUT THE AUTHOR

Phillip Strang was born in England in the late forties, during the post-war baby boom. He had a comfortable middle-class upbringing, spending his childhood years in a small town seventy miles west of London.

His childhood and the formative years were a time of innocence. There were relatively few rules, and as a teenager he had complete freedom, thanks to a bicycle – a three-speed Raleigh. It was in the days before mobile phones, the internet, terrorism and wanton violence. He was an avid reader of science fiction in his teenage years: Isaac Asimov, Frank Herbert, the masters of the genre. Much of what they and others mentioned has now become a reality. Science fiction has now become science fact. Still an avid reader, the author now mainly reads thrillers.

In his early twenties, the author, with a degree in electronics engineering and a desire to see the world, left the cold, damp climes of England for Sydney, Australia – his first semi-circulation of the globe. Now, forty years later, he still resides in Australia, although many intervening years were spent in a myriad of countries, some calm and safe, others no more than war zones.

Made in the USA
San Bernardino, CA
05 July 2018